HIS BEAUTIFUL REVENGE

A BILLIONAIRE ROMANCE

MICHELLE LOVE

HOT AND STEAMY ROMANCE

CONTENTS

Blurb	1
1. Chapter One	3
2. Chapter Two	14
3. Chapter Three	23
4. Chapter Four	34
5. Chapter Five	41
6. Chapter Six	49
7. Chapter Seven	59
8. Chapter Eight	68
9. Chapter Nine	82
10. Chapter Ten	96
11. Chapter Eleven	111
12. Chapter Twelve	127
13. Chapter Thirteen	139
14. Chapter Fourteen	155
15. Chapter Fifteen	173
16. Chapter Sixteen	195
17. Chzpter Seventeen	204
18. Chapter Eighteen	218
About the Author	229

Made in "The United States" by:

Michelle Love

© Copyright 2021

ISBN: 978-1-64808-075-3

ALL RIGHTS RESERVED. No part of this publication may be reproduced or transmitted in any form whatsoever, electronic, or mechanical, including photocopying, recording, or by any informational storage or retrieval system without express written, dated and signed permission from the author

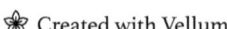 Created with Vellum

BLURB

So, you think I have it all? Yes, I'm Giacomo Conti, the billionaire. Dark Italian good looks, sex appeal, and every woman I meet practically begging to get me into bed? That's my world, yes.

So why am I in a loveless relationship with a gold-digging woman who cheats on me every chance she gets?
Enough is enough.
That's why I hired Norah. My sweet, beautiful, tender, delectable Norah.
It wasn't meant to go anywhere. She was supposed to help me catch my cheater of a girlfriend and her abusive ex, in the middle of their affair.
But it went so much further.

I know she'll be a challenge, I know it won't be easy.
But I'm Giacomo Conti.
She doesn't stand a chance...

Norah, a beautiful, young graphic designer, is convinced her boyfriend **Lucian** is having an affair but as yet hasn't been able to prove it. Miserable in her relationship, she throws herself into her work, and through it, meets an enigmatic billionaire, **Giacomo,** who hires her to design the marketing campaign for his new tech. There is an instant attraction, but Norah is determined not to sink to Lucian's level and denies herself, even when Giacomo makes it clear he wants her.

Meanwhile, after a terrible tragedy, Giacomo is trying to convince his best friend, **Orlando,** a single father to a young daughter, to get back into the dating game. Lando is unenthusiastic ...until he meets **Zulika,** a feisty young photographer with whom he bonds. But Zulika has her own demons to overcome, not less the fractured relationship with her brother, Lucian, who is cheating on Zulika's best friend, Norah.

When she finally discovers the truth about Lucian's infidelity, she is shocked to find his lover is supermodel **Tara Hubert**—Giacomo's fiancée. Realizing that Giacomo has also discovered the affair, she starts to spend more time with him after they both end their relationships. Soon, things become sexual and Norah wonders how she could ever have settled for anyone less than this gorgeous, sensual man.

But both Lucian and Tara are infuriated by the discovery of their betrayal and both plot their revenge in very different ways —ways that may split apart more than just one couple. Can Norah and Giacomo's love survive the ferocity of their ex lovers' anger, and just how far will Tara and Lucian go?

1

CHAPTER ONE

The phone's shrill ring broke across the bookstore. Zulika waved the receiver.

"Lucian," she yelled across the room. Norah didn't notice the man sitting at the corner table and the way he stiffened at Zulika's words, his attention caught. Norah grinned at Zulika as she took the phone from her.

"I've told you before, me Norah, him Lucian."

Zulika poked her tongue out good-naturedly at her friend.

"Ha ha." She walked away, swatting Norah's butt with her hand.

"Hey, you," Norah glanced at the clock on the wall of the bookshop.

"Hey, doll," Lucian sang cheerfully. "It's Friday, work's out, and I'm in the mood for some quality time with you. Are you going home soon?"

Norah grinned, caught up in his mood. He sounded more cheerful than he had in months. And wanting to spend time alone with her? Rare, she thought to herself, what was up with him? But she didn't want to waste his good humor.

"Yeah, very soon. Just gotta clear up some stuff-then I'm all yours. You cooking?"

They both laughed. "Pizza it is, then," Norah said. "I'll pick it up on the way home. Do we have beer?"

There was a pause. "Well, we did until last night."

She rolled her eyes. "Okay. Hey, did Ziggy eat his breakfast?" Ziggy was their ancient St. Bernard crossed with a barrel on legs. Lately he had stopped eating so much.

"Yep, all of it." Lucian sounded like a proud daddy.

"Oh, good. O Okay, be home soon."

"Love you."

She hesitated, then smiled. "Love you too."

NORAH WENT BACK UP to her little office above the bookshop. Her freelance graphic design company—consisting of just Norah and her uber-organized work ethic—was beginning to take off and she found herself spending less time in the bookstore she ran with her almost-sister-in-law and best friend, Zulika. It was a blessing and a curse, she thought now as she glanced through the endless emails she'd received. As much as her first love was art and design, she loved the laid-back pace and friendly atmosphere of their San Francisco store. Now that Russian Hill was an up and coming "hip" area, their clientele had tripled in the three years they had been open. The store, all dark wood bookshelves and large, comfortable couches, had added a coffee machine in the last year, which had drawn many people in, and they had recently expanded into the empty store front next door, adding tables where writers could sit and work. Ziggy also took up residence, making friends with the customers and their dogs.

Norah, at twenty-eight, was completing her Ph.D. in graphic design part-time as well as working, and sometimes the work seemed overwhelming. She wondered if she had missed the signs that her relationship of five years with Lucian Hargity was beginning to unravel and whether it was her fault for working too hard. She'd even said as much to Zulika—Lucian's stepsister—but Zulika had merely rolled her eyes. "If my brother can't handle a successful woman, that's on him, not you."

Zulika and Lucian were not close, but Norah and Zulika were, and so Zulika put up with her brother. Her mother had married Lucian's father after both being widowed, but the marriage had been a disaster and lasted less than five years. It had cost Zulika's mother her health and when she died, Zulika went to her best friend for comfort: Norah. The two had met in college and become as close as sisters; they'd earned the name "the twins" because they were always together. Looks-wise, the only thing they shared was their long, dark hair. Norah, with her dark beauty inherited from her Indian mother, dark brown eyes, and soft, warm smile, was tall and curvaceous, whereas Zulika, her sapphire-blue eyes large behind black-rimmed spectacles, was athletic and slender. They shared a silly sense of humor as well as sharp intelligence and street-smarts. Despite never being apart for long, they enjoyed each other's company.

Norah considered Zulika her family and when she had met her step-brother, Lucian, it seemed the orphaned Norah had found her family. It was only later that she discovered that Zulika had been dismayed at the relationship between her best friend and step-brother. It had bugged her ever since, but to Zulika's credit, she had never bad-mouthed Lucian to Norah or interfered in their relationship.

Five years later, and Norah felt as if something major—something bad—was about to happen. Lucian had been distant, distracted, and even cold. They rarely made love anymore, both exhausted from work. Lucian worked for a major PR company in the Bay Area and his work often took him down to Los Angeles or over to New York. Yes, that was it, Norah told herself, it was work ...except ...She knew from Zulika that Lucian was relatively junior in his role. At thirty-one and not long out of college—where he had struggled to maintain higher marks—he was still working his way up the ladder. Norah wondered if all of his trips were actually work and not ...

No. Stop thinking about it. An affair? Norah was horrified by her own thought process. She would rather think the worst of him than accept that his trips were genuine. It wasn't fair to Lucian. But she couldn't shake the feeling that he was treading water with her.

She pushed the thought out of her mind—something she had a lot of practice with—and it wasn't until there was a soft knock on the door that she looked up from her work. The sun was getting low in the window and, for August, that meant it was getting late.

"Yes?"

The door opened and Lucian stuck his dark blonde head around it. "Hey, you."

Norah was surprised. "Hey ...I thought I was meeting you at home."

"I thought I would surprise you—and say hi to my little sister. She's serving a customer, so I thought I'd come up."

"The store's still open ...sorry. I mean, hi," she chuckled and kissed him. Lucian was a typical preppy archetype—handsome, well-maintained ...bland. What had attracted her to him in the first place ...Norah was ashamed that she couldn't remember, but she knew she had loved him once. Now ...didn't all relationships turn into this? Friends with benefits? If you could describe their stale sex life as a benefit.

They went back downstairs to see Zulika finally locking the store up. She grinned at Norah, half-ignoring her stepbrother.

"You will not believe the sale I just made; that complete leather-bound Dickens collection? Sold, baby."

Norah's jaw dropped. "The five-thousand dollar set?"

"The very one."

"Holy moly …we've had that for years."

Zulika grinned at Norah. "You wanna make out with me?"

"Always."

"Okay, it just got weird." Lucian pretended to be sick.

"Yeah, but if I wasn't your sister …"

"Dude, stop. You really have no filter, huh?"

Zulika shook her head. "Nah. Not much of one. By the way, I have news. I have a date."

Lucian and Norah looked at each other, then at Zulika.

"Holy hell." Norah's eyes were wide.

"Did the skies darken?" Lucian checked outside the window.

"Oh, you're both so fucking funny." Zulika gave them both the finger, but she grinned and chuckled.

"When's the first date?"

"Tomorrow night. Oh, I was going to ask a huge favor." Zulika fluttered her eyelashes at Norah. "It would be really nice if, say, I at least attempted to look like a lady. And seeing as I don't own anything …"

Norah smiled. Zulika was always borrowing from Norah's beloved collection of vintage dresses and Norah kept a few of them upstairs in her office for "emergencies" just like this one. "Yes. Here." She threw her door key to Zulika. "Go nuts. Just don't wreck it."

Zulika kissed her cheek. "You're the best."

She and Lucian laughed at the speed with which Zulika scooted out of the door. Lucian shook his head.

"Poor guy doesn't stand a chance."

Norah grinned. "Who is it anyways? Not Rufus?" She looked hopeful and Lucian grinned.

"You wish, Reddy. How long have you been trying to finagle that? Two, three years?"

Norah tapped her head. "I'm telling you, it'll happen. I know things."

Lucian hooted. "Oh, you know things. Tell me, O Wise One, why do you want them to get together?"

"Because they are perfect for each other. Zulika is gorgeous, Rufus is cute, and he makes her laugh."

Lucian's smile was fond—and a little patronizing. "Is that really all you look for in a man?"

Norah flushed at the slight. "That ...along with kindness and fidelity." She couldn't resist the snark and she watched something flicker in Lucian's eyes. He didn't rise to the bait though. "Come on, you. Let's get home to the dog. Both he and I are starving."

Norah relented a little. "I can rustle up dog-food pizza for both of you?"

Lucian laughed. "Yum. Now I'm really hungry."

"Gross."

That made him laugh even harder. "Let's see, do I fancy beef chunks in gravy? Chicken in jelly?"

Norah made a gagging face. "Stop, please." He laughed, caught her by the waist, and pulled her into his arms, kissing her tenderly. It was a sweet, loving kiss, but Norah felt herself tense up. Lucian noticed and his smile faded.

"Let's go. I'm bushed." He walked out of the door in front of her and got into his own car, not waiting for her to follow him on the way back to their Palo Alto home.

For a brief second, Norah considered not going home, staying there, pulling out the little temporary cot they kept upstairs for emergencies, and sleeping there. If it wasn't for Ziggy ...

Norah sighed and, starting her car, followed Lucian out of the city.

GIACOMO CONTI WAS BORED. Yet another cocktail party with people he had nothing in common with, yet another evening wasted when he could be working, or reading, or hanging out with his own, more sedate friends. But then again, he reasoned, Tara was willing to appear with him for public events whenever he needed her, so it was only fair. He looked across at her now, seeing her blonde hair falling to her shoulders, her petite, doll-like features, and her long, long legs. Tara Hubert was the world's highest-paid supermodel and she was with him. Giacomo Conti was a self-made billionaire, an Italian geek whose brilliance within the technology field had sent his career into the stratosphere when he was just nineteen.

Almost half a lifetime and now he was bored. His company, Conti-Tech, was competing with the Googles and Facebooks of the world and was on target to be a trillion-dollar company any day now. Yet Giacomo found himself envious of the lives his friends led—more sedate and less shallow. As teachers, writers, artist, and lawyers, they didn't work any less hard for what they had; it was just their fields didn't pay as much, apart from the lucky few. Giacomo's best friend and his brother in arms, Orlando Price, was a school teacher in one of the city's poorest schools, and yet the results he had with his kids, the hope and inspiration he imparted, was priceless. Giacomo's evenings with Orlando, his wife, Carmel, and their seven-year-old daughter, Ferma, were his absolute favorite times. Tara never joined them. She had little time for the "little" people, and she and Carmel had no time for each other whatsoever. Tara's beauty was icy and cold, whereas Carmel's dark good looks were sensual and exciting. Tara was jealous, so when Giacomo insisted on spending time with his friends, Tara always cried off—to everyone's relief.

And now …Giacomo realized he hadn't been listening to the

man talking to him, but there was a good reason. Tara was cheating on him. Giacomo had suspected it for months and now he had a name to go with his suspicions: Lucian Hargity. Giacomo had had his private detectives follow Tara for the last three months, document and photograph every time she met with the man, and build a portfolio that, when Giacomo confronted her, Tara would not be able to deny.

It had been Carmel who had started him thinking. She'd mentioned she'd seen Tara in the city with another man months previously, not realizing that Tara had told Giacomo that she would be in New York for work. Carmel had been horrified to think she had casually blurted out the evidence of Tara's cheating, but Giacomo had reassured her it had been for the best. Carmel had shaken her head angrily.

"Giacomo, I know it shouldn't be my business, but don't ever bring that woman here again. I don't take her cheating on you lightly."

There had been a nasty incident a few weeks later when the two women had come face-to-face. Carmel had to be restrained by her husband as Tara bitched at her about Giacomo's emersion in work, and she couldn't help blurting out that at least Giacomo knew about loyalty. Tara had asked her what she meant by that and Carmel had snarled at her. "You know."

Giacomo had feigned innocence when Tara asked him about it and Carmel had apologized to Giacomo for her mouth. "It gets away from me sometimes," she said ruefully, hugging him. "I just can't stand the fact that she had the nerve to cheat on you."

Giacomo had hugged her tightly. "Don't worry, Bella. I'll handle it."

Since then, he had bided his time, burying himself in work as his detectives gathered the evidence. Only today he had been at a meeting—completely disengaged—that afterward he had decided to go to the workplace of Hargity's girlfriend and sister.

He had donned a baseball cap over his dark curls and stuck some Wayfarers on his face to cover his distinctive green eyes.

At thirty-seven, Giacomo Conti was considered one of the world's handsomest, most eligible (said the women's magazines, choosing to forget his relationship with Tara) bachelors. His tall, darkly handsome face was saved from being generic by the brooding, almost dangerous set of his green eyes rimmed by thick, black lashes, his chin dimple, and his strong jaw. His black hair was left to grow in wild curls, and he was a man who could make both a Saville Row suit and an Abercrombie and Fitch sweater look good. His broad shoulders, slim hips, and long legs contributed to his demeanor, and on the rare occasion that he smiled, it lit up the room.

Giacomo knew he was good looking and did not believe in false modesty. When he was younger, he had screwed his way across Italy, then Europe, and finally, the world. His sexual prowess was legendary. Giacomo deliberately let the world think he was a playboy and as deep as a puddle. It suited him to know that the real Giacomo was still that little geek playing with computers in his small house in Trani. His small circle of "real" friends knew him as "Jack" and knew the fun-loving, loyal, big-hearted man beneath the image. He trusted few people with the truth ...especially not women.

So, when Tara's infidelity came to light, he hadn't been that shocked. And today, when he'd gone to the little bookshop, Anthology, in the Russian Hill district, he had been pleasantly surprised at the laid-back feel and the friendliness. The giant St. Bernard had taken a shine to him and sat with him as he drank the superb coffee and watched the two women who ran the shop. Giacomo could barely take his eyes off the taller woman, Tara's lover's girlfriend. Her sweet smile, her easy, infectious laughter, her patient way with customers, and her literary knowledge spoke to Giacomo in a way he'd never felt.

He's cheating on you, lovely girl? Idiot, he thought in disbelief. When the phone had rung and the younger woman had yelled out the bastard's name, Giacomo had felt immediately on edge—almost jealous, almost wanting to yell at her to ignore it and that the figlio di puttana wasn't good enough for her. He'd watched her face break into a smile and couldn't do it. He couldn't break this lovely girl's heart.

He'd left soon after, unable to stand it. At home, he hadn't been able to resist Googling her. Norah Reddy, part owner of The Anthology Bookstore and also a freelance graphic designer. He looked through her online portfolio and was impressed. He called Sebastien, his longtime personal assistant, and asked him to set up a meeting with her. "I think we might find her useful for the some of the campaigns we have coming up," He told Seb. Also, she's gorgeous and I want to see her again. He grinned to himself as he hung up. Two birds with one stone. If he could harness the woman's obvious talent and get that beautiful body into his bed ...opportunity and revenge in one go.

He smiled to himself again now as the cocktail party droned on. Watching Tara network and flirt with the men in the room (Giacomo knew Tara barely registered the other women, knowing she was the most beautiful woman there), he wondered how he had ever gotten involved with her. She was so totally opposite of what he was attracted to, but then again, five years ago he'd been reeling from the death of his grandparents—cancer, within weeks of each other—and he'd dealt with it by drinking and numbing the pain by screwing around. Tara had seen his sadness and moved in, telling him she was what he needed.

He felt a pang of sadness now. Yes, he had needed her then and he couldn't help but know that he was partially responsible for the fracture in their relationship now. He was obsessed with his work and passionate about what he could achieve. He had neglected her and Tara wasn't a woman to neglect. He'd seen the disgust in her eyes when she looked at him. Maybe he should just cut her free.

His phone beeped—a message from Orlando. Dinner with Carmel and me, Friday?

Giacomo smiled. "Yes, god, please." Hell, yes. Send black-ops to get me out of this party.

Ha ha. Grit your teeth. See you Friday, buddy.

Giacomo sighed. What he wouldn't give to have a time machine now. Still, he had no meetings tomorrow as yet ...so he could always go spend some time in that little bookshop ...

He pushed the thought away and went to get his drink refilled.

CHAPTER TWO

Carmel gently took the headphones off her sleeping husband's head. Orlando was stretched lengthways on their couch, his breath coming out in tiny snores. She kissed his forehead and smoothed a finger down his face. His arm, solid and muscular, slipped from his chest and hit the floor. He stirred, grumbled softly, and turned onto his side, still muttering. Carmel suppressed a laugh. She moved around the living room, picking up empty bottles, cups, sheet music, and student papers. It was a wonder any students got the correct papers back from their favorite music teacher. Orlando's organization skills were not exactly a gift. Carmel stacked everything that looked school-related carefully on the small desk in the corner of the room, catching them as they slipped out of her grip.

As she tidied, she glanced out the window of their small home and froze. A movement caught her eye—someone moving away from the window. Their neighborhood was safe and it shook her to see that. Not least because, for the last few weeks, she had had a creeping feeling that she was being followed or watched. Carmel wasn't a woman who scared easily, but it had been insidious, and whenever she had been alone, out in the city or on her way to work, she had become more paranoid. She hadn't said anything to Orlando, not wanting to worry him until she knew for sure.

Now, though, if whoever was following her—if they actually existed—was coming to her house ...No. No way, buster. Not with my daughter asleep upstairs.

She opened the front door and stepped out onto the porch, peering into the gloom. The street—which was tree-lined and still somewhere the kids could play outside—was empty, except for Jason, the elderly man down the street, who waved at her. She waved back, smiling. Jason was in a wheelchair and hardly likely to be peering in their high windows.

Satisfied she was being paranoid, she turned and went inside. Just for once, she locked both doors. She heard footsteps and turned. Orlando shuffled sleepily from the living room. He ran a hand through his short hair and grinned at her.

""Sup, babe, what you ..." he yawned expansively, " ...doing out there?" He took in her face. She was frowning slightly. "What's the matter?" He stepped toward her and slid his arms around her waist. Carmel blinked and her face cleared.

"Ah, nothing," she said, not convincing him for a second. "Well, I just thought I saw someone watching the house. But there wasn't. So." He grinned down at her, cheeky and boyish. "Shut up." She scowled at him, trying not to smile

"Watching the house?"

"Shut up." She started to laugh. Orlando put a mock-serious look on his face.

"No, no, no, better to make sure. Want me to have a look ..."

"...no ..."

"...wouldn't hurt to look." He reached behind her and opened the door. For a second they both looked out. Carmel secretly hoped they would see ...something.

Orlando turned to look at her. "Hmmm, strange ..." She wiggled away from him, swiping at him. Laughing, he gathered her up in his arms and buried his face in her neck, pressing his lips against her warm skin. He felt her body relax and, raising his head, tipped her face up to his. He kissed her gently on the mouth. Carmel sighed with happiness.

"Wanna go cuddle some?" He muttered, his lips moving against hers. She responded by kissing him harder. His right hand tangled in her hair as their kiss deepened, his left hand sliding down the curve of her back. She pressed her body into his, feeling the excitement build in both their bodies. She gasped for air as he broke away, sliding his hands under her buttocks and lifting her so her legs curled around his back. His dark brown eyes burned with desire as he bore her up the stairs.

He laid her on the bed and was undressing her when they heard it. "Ah," said Orlando, sighing. "The walking, talking contraceptive device."

Mommy! Carmel chuckled and disengaged herself from her husband. "Take a load off. I'll go see what she wants."

"There's a reason you don't have brothers or sisters," Orlando yelled grumpily to his daughter and Carmel hushed him, giggling as she went to see what her daughter wanted.

Ferma was sitting up in bed, her hair in cornrows. "What is it, sweetie?"

"Monster."

Carmel sighed. "Where, darling?"

"On my toes."

"A monster on your toes. Okay." Carmel sat down, pretending to look under the comforter. "Now, who would be so brave to go near your stinky feet, punkin'?" She lifted the edge of the comforter, then pretended to hold her nose. "Pooh! No, no monster, darling. No cheesy feet-eating monster."

Ferma giggled and wiggled her toes. "My feet don't stink."

"They don't? Okay, I'll check again ...pooh, arghhhh!" Carmel pretended to choke on the 'stink.' "Help, I can't breathe ...the smell! The smell!"

Ferma giggled uncontrollably and Carmel tickled her daughter. "Now look, kiddo, there are no monsters, okay? None that will get in here—not while I'm around. Okay, Snugglepuss? Sleepy time now."

She settled Ferma back into her blankets, then went back to bed to find Orlando sprawled across the bed, snoring. "So much for love," she muttered, grinning, then crawled into bed next to him and was asleep almost as soon as she closed her eyes.

NORAH SHUT off the shower and dressed quickly. Lucian lay watching her, then, as she passed him, hooked her legs and pulled her down onto the bed.

"Stay, stay," he said, pinning her down. She wriggled out from underneath him, annoyed.

"Quit it! Too much to do. Get off, get off." She struggled to her feet and swatted his head, smiling to soften the snub. "Up, up. Time to do manly stuff." Lucian rolled into a sitting position, yawned and smiled at her.

"Manly stuff?"

She grinned. "Yep. Chop wood, hunt bison, that kinda stuff."

From downstairs, they heard a pitiful whimper—Ziggy wanted his breakfast.

Norah sighed.

"I gotta feed the kid." She left Lucian to shower and thumped downstairs. Ziggy was beside himself. She fought him off while reaching for his food, his nose seeking out the meaty chunks. As soon as she put his bowl on the floor, Ziggy fell on it with abandon.

Norah switched on the coffee pot and surveyed the contents of the fridge. Eggs. Eggs sounded good. She snagged a mixing bowl from the cupboard, feeling the satisfying crack of the shell against her palm. She grimaced as the egg white stuck to her skin and flicked the food into the bowl. She was whisking the eggs, adding some paprika, when Lucian came down the stairs.

Ziggy had finished his food and was now licking the empty bowl around the kitchen, the metal scraping against the floor tile. Lucian snatched up the bowl and Ziggy looked up at him with hope.

"Now you've done it," Norah shook her head. "He thinks he's getting extra."

Lucian shrugged. "No dice, dog," he addressed Ziggy, "Live with it." He threw the dish into the sink. Ziggy harrumphed and wandered off. Lucian grinned and slid his hands around Norah's waist, pretending to bite her neck.

She put the bowl of eggs into the microwave, fixed the time, and pressed start. She turned to face him.

"Boobie check." Lucian pulled her shirt out and peered down her cleavage. "Yep, still there." She half-smiled, a little irritated by his cheerfulness. Norah was not a morning person.

Lucian smiled. "You okay?"

"Yeah, fine. Do you want eggs?"

"Please."

They were interrupted by the sound of wood being chewed. Lucian grabbed Ziggy and tugged him away from the table.

"Hey, hey, quit that." Ziggy grumbled, rolling onto his back and biting his own leg, wiggling his body from side to side. Lucian laughed at their dog, teasing him with his toys and playing tug of war. "Stupid mutt."

"Don't call him stupid," Norah said and bent to kiss Ziggy's head. "You're Mummy's favorite boy. Yes, you are." Ziggy licked her face and she giggled.

The microwave beeped. At the same time, a knock came from the front door. Norah threw Lucian the dish cloth.

"I'll get the door. You deal with breakfast."

"Okay. I'll let his majesty out for a run. He's antsy."

The postman was waiting with a package for Norah to sign. She thanked him and was opening it when Lucian came back into the kitchen. "Anything interesting?"

Norah was studying the contents—a Conti-Tech brochure and letter outlining their future projects. The letter, by the looks of it handwritten by Giacomo Conti himself, asked her to keep the contents secret and requested she call his private office to set up a meeting.

I HAVE STUDIED YOUR PORTFOLIO, Miss Reddy, and I think we can work well together. I'd like to hear your vision and see if we can build a professional relationship.

Look forward to hearing from you very soon.

Yours,

Giacomo Conti

NORAH FELT HER BODY TREMBLE. Conti-Tech wanted her? She felt a little breathless. If she landed a Conti-Tech contract ...god, it would send her career into the stratosphere. "Just a possible future client," she said casually, stuffing the contents back into the envelope and slipping it into her bag. "Nothing interesting."

As they ate breakfast, Norah asked herself when she had stopped confiding in Lucian about the important things in her life. Then it struck her. Had she ever? Had she ever trusted him? She studied him now. "How's work?"

Lucian shrugged. "Busy. Too many egos at work on this latest job. I tell you, never work with diva photographers or supermodels. A nightmare to work with. It doesn't matter what we've pitched; they always, always change their minds. You're lucky in your line of work."

"Yes," Norah said dryly. "Because clients never change their minds in my line of work."

He waved away her sarcasm with his hand. "You know what I mean. You don't have the high-pressure work that I do."

Norah gritted her teeth. This was more like it. The affable, fun-loving boyfriend of this morning was gone and in his place, the egotistical douchebag who belittled her at every turn. Her eyes narrowed at him. "Why do you do that?"

"What?"

"Put me down? Does it make you feel like more of a man?"

"What the hell are you talking about?"

"You don't have the high-pressure work I do." She mimicked him, knowing it annoyed him. "I run my own business, Lucian, and you think I don't have pressure? Actually, I run two businesses. So don't give me that bullshit."

Lucian looked astonished at her outburst. Finally, he started to smile. "Are you menstruating?"

Wanting to pound the smirk off his face, Norah got up. "I'm going to work." She looked around for her phone, and realizing she'd left it upstairs, she headed out of the door.

Upstairs, she sat on the bed and took a deep breath in. Why was she so annoyed? Maybe because this is what Lucian did—he'd be playful, friendly when it suited him, and distant and dismissive when it didn't. She was sick of it. She dropped her head in her hands. It was Saturday and she was glad that she had the bookstore to open. Maybe it would distract her. She grabbed her phone, then saw her pill packet next to the glass of water on her nightstand. God, she'd forgotten to take it this morning. Hurriedly, she swallowed it with some water. *No, Lucian, I'm not on my period because I make sure I never have* them. She didn't question why she had always made absolutely sure she wouldn't get pregnant ...not with Lucian's child. As she walked back downstairs, she asked herself the same question she had asked herself for a long time now ...

Why the hell am I still with him?

LUCIAN HEARD her on the stairs and stuffed the envelope back into her bag. Conti-Tech. Giacomo Conti wanted to hire Norah. Coincidence? He didn't think so. Norah came in and grabbed her bag, giving him a short, "See you later." He grunted in reply, then when he heard the front door close, he pulled his cellphone out.

Tara's greeting was a purr, but a few seconds later she was much less friendly. "What the fuck are you talking about?"

"I'm talking about your boyfriend hiring my girlfriend. Does he know about us?"

"No, of course not. How could he?"

Lucian sighed. "I thought you said that friend of his might have seen us."

"Carmel? That situation is being dealt with. Put it out of your mind."

"How do you mean 'dealt with?'"

"Don't worry about it. I don't think this thing with Giacomo and your girlfriend is anything to worry about. Didn't you tell me she was an excellent graphic designer?"

"Well, yes ..."

"Giacomo has a habit of nurturing new talent. He probably just sent out feelers to a whole slew of young up-and-comers. If we freak out about it ...well, that's just going to confirm issues."

Lucian rubbed his eyes. "When can I see you?"

"Soon. As soon as this other situation is over with." Tara's voice warmed again. "I'll miss you. I'll miss your cock inside me, baby. I'll miss sucking it …"

"God," Lucian gave a moan of desire. "I want to cum inside you so hard, beautiful …"

She laughed softly. "I'll be thinking about you …"

CHAPTER THREE

Norah read and re-read Giacomo Conti's letter. She showed it to an impressed Zulika, whose eyes bugged out of their sockets. "Wow. I mean, wow, Norah."

"I know, right?"

It was late afternoon and the bookstore was quiet for once. Norah couldn't resist telling Zulika about the letter. Zulika read Giacomo's handwritten letter and sighed. "Even his handwriting is sexy."

"He's sexy?" Norah looked confused. She'd never seen the man himself. Zulika rolled her eyes.

"Just occasionally," she teased, "Check out some gossip sites instead of your usual geeky ones. Here," she grabbed her iPad and quickly brought up some photos. She handed it to Norah, who did a double-take.

"Holy moly." She looked into the intense green eyes and dark good looks of Giacomo Conti. "I thought he was much older."

"Well?"

Norah nodded, grinning. "That is one gorgeous man."

"And you could be working closely with him," Zulika teased,

"I can see it now …you're working one late night, on an urgent presentation. You're both so absorbed in the work that you don't realize it's gotten dark outside. You lean across him and he smells your perfume…"

Norah was giggling. "Are you writing some kind of porn movie in your head?"

"Hey, you mentioned porn, so who's the pervert?" Zulika grinned and Norah flushed. She'd got her there. Norah held up the iPad, trying to hide her embarrassment.

"Look at this man. Who wouldn't think of porn?"

"True story."

Grinning, Norah handed her back her tablet. "Anyway, besides that, it could mean the business taking off."

"Which might mean you not being free to work here as much." Zulika nodded, "I get it. We always thought that might happen."

"Do you mind?"

Zulika shook her head. "Putting aside the fact I'll miss your company, your business is the reason our business has been financed this long. I'm grateful. I'm more than that; I'm delighted for you. We need to celebrate."

"Good idea."

Zulika studied her friend. "Why don't you stay with me tonight? Call Luc, tell him you need a girl's night in."

Norah nodded. "I'd like that." What she didn't add was it would be a relief. The tension at home and Lucian's mood swings—she needed a break from it. What she also hadn't told anyone else was that she'd been looking at apartments in the city to rent. If Lucian was cheating, then she already knew her plan. In a weird way, she almost hoped he was cheating because then she would have the final push to do what she had wanted to do for a long time.

End it.

Giacomo had now been to the Anthology three times and was feeling like somethings of a stalker. Finally Seb had told him that Norah Reddy had called and tomorrow was the day he would finally meet her. The few hours he had spent in her unknowing company, he had seen a woman who, above all else, was free. Free from vanity and free from expectations. He reminded himself that he did not really know her from those hours observing her, but he couldn't help feeling excited about the meeting.

Tonight, however, Tara was sitting out on his balcony, smoking one cigarette after another and fretting about ...what was it this time? Giacomo sighed and went outside, pinching a cigarette from her packet.

"What is wrong today?" He said, lighting the cigarette and inhaling deeply. He studied her. Tara, her denim-blue eyes large, was almost thirty, but she looked a good five years older. Sun damage and smoking had weathered her face, but it didn't detract from her beauty. She gazed back at him steadily.

"Why have you never asked me to marry you?"

The question surprised Giacomo. They had never discussed marriage before. He leaned forward. "Because marriage has never figured into my plans," he said honestly. "And, rightly or wrongly, I thought you would prefer to have a career rather than be shackled to me."

And why would I marry someone who would cheat on me? Or is that why you are cheating on me?

Tara smirked. "My career is steady. I get the work of girls ten years younger."

"I know that you do."

"But I think of marriage, kids ..."

"With me?"

Tara put out her cigarette. "Of course you."

Giacomo smiled coolly. "I'm surprised."

"Why?"

He met her gaze steadily, leaving the reason unspoken. Tara was the first to look away. "Whatever."

She got up, but he caught her hand. "You are not happy, Tara."

"No."

"Then why don't you leave?"

She didn't answer, merely pulling her hand away. As she turned to leave, he saw, just for a moment, a flash of hurt in her eyes.

"Tara ..."

"Don't," she said, her voice quivering, and disappeared back into the apartment. Giacomo felt like a heel, but told himself he'd done nothing wrong. *You're not the one who is cheating.*

"Not yet," he said, thinking of Norah Reddy's pink lips and sweet smile. "Not yet." He dropped his head into his hands and sighed.

Che cazzo di casino. What a fucking mess.

NORAH STRAIGHTENED her skirt over her hips and wished she had another suit. As a graphic designer, she'd always been casually, if professionally, dressed, but otherwise she was hardly ever out of jeans and Chuck Taylor's. She felt awkward in the dark red suit, but as soon as Giacomo Conti entered the room, she forgot everything else. The photograph on the website did not do him justice.

He shook her hand, his large, warm hand dwarfing hers, and led her into his office. His very cute assistant, Sebastien, grinned at her.

"Would you like some coffee?"

"Just water, please," she managed to croak out at him and he gave a reassuring wink.

"Jack, for you?"

Giacomo smiled and Norah felt her stomach flip. God ...that smile. "Water's good for me too. Thanks, Seb."

"He's nice," Norah said after Seb had gone and Giacomo smiled.

"He is, and very efficient. I got lucky. Now, I want to thank you for coming to see me, Norah—I can call you Norah, yes?"

Oh, god, yes. Especially with the accent. "Of course, Mr. Conti."

He laughed. "And that's "Jack" to you. I hate standing on formality."

Norah relaxed a little. "Me too."

"Good. Now, as I said in my letter, we have a number of new projects in the pipeline and I was impressed with your portfolio."

Norah nodded. "And thank you for taking the time to look, but, Mr. Conti, I have to tell you from the off: I've never worked a major project before. Not that I wouldn't welcome the chance to work with you, but I have to be honest. It would be a huge step-up for me."

"I appreciate that," Giacomo—Jack, she reminded herself—said as Seb came in with their drinks. "Then, I suppose, think of this as graduation day." He grinned at Seb, who rolled his eyes.

"That's his favorite saying," Seb said to Norah in a stage-whisper and she chuckled.

"It is?"

Giacomo nodded. "Yes, but it's also true. Norah, Seb's right in that I do like to nurture new talent, especially from the Bay Area, but it helps when that talent has new, fresh, exciting ideas ...and your portfolio shows me how talented you are."

Seb made a loud beeping noise. "Too many uses of the word 'talent.' You're out."

"You're fired," Giacomo shot back, grinning, as Seb made his exit, laughing out loud. Norah was shaking her head in disbelief at the comedy show.

"I may be out of line, but I've never been in an office like this," she laughed and Giacomo smiled at her.

"Like I said, I hate formality. Or hierarchies. God, who gets off on power trips? Never a good way to run a business."

Norah liked this man –immensely—not just because his green eyes were beautiful and warm or because his smile was making a steady pulse beat between her legs, but because, if nothing else, he was honest. Rich, handsome, the world at his feet, but he made jokes with his employees and took their teasing with good humor. Yeah, you're a good one, Norah thought and felt sadness that she didn't know more men like him.

"Are you okay?"

She pulled herself up. "Yes, very. Just wishing more workplaces were like this."

He smiled. "I hear you. Come and sit on the balcony and we'll talk about the projects I have in mind."

THE AFTERNOON FLEW by and Norah left the Conti building feeling more energized by work than she had for a long time. The challenges Giacomo Conti laid in front of her were daunting in their scope, to be sure, but the kind of challenge she had longed for.

"I see us working closely together," he said, his eyes twinkling, and she grinned at his flirtatious manner; this man knew how gorgeous he was and didn't mind using it. You are trouble, she thought now, smiling to herself, but she had enjoyed every moment in Giacomo Conti's company. More than his looks and personality, though, he had treated her with respect, listened to her as she went through some preliminary ideas, and gave her constructive criticism and praise. It had been a productive, collaborative meeting and she had enjoyed it. Giacomo had asked her to officially sign a contract with him. She had agreed without even discussing money; she had forgotten all about the money side of thing until she got home and read through the contract.

She frowned. It must be a typo. She grabbed her phone and called him. "I think there's been a typo," she said, her tone amused. "There are one too many zeros on the end of this check."

She heard his deep, soft laugh and it sent thrills through her. "No," he said. "There's no mistake."

Norah gasped. "Giacomo ...no. This is too generous."

"No, it isn't. You just haven't been paid what you are clearly worth before. I have to tell –you—I won't budge on this."

Norah was speechless. "I don't know what to say except thank you for believing in me."

That laugh again. "I know you won't let me down."

"I won't. I promise. Not ever." Were they still talking about work? The conversation had taken a far more intimate turn and Norah felt her body quiver with longing.

There was a pause in the conversation. "Norah ...I'm having dinner with some friends tomorrow night. Would you like to join me?"

Norah felt a pang. God, yes, she would but ... "Giacomo, I can't. I'm sorry. I have commitments at home."

"Understood. Another time?"

"Definitely. Goodnight, Giacomo."

"Sweet dreams, Bella."

. . .

SHE COULDN'T STOP THINKING about him. She went to bed that night, and as Lucian was still out, she allowed herself a little fantasy, sliding her hand between her legs and stroking her clit as she conjured up an image of Giacomo Conti naked, wet from the shower as he opened the door to her. He smiled, saying nothing, but pulling her gently into his arms. Norah gave a soft moan as she imagined his lips against hers, his strong hands sliding under her dress to tug her panties down her legs. She bit her lip as her hand moved faster on her clit and she imagined his cock, huge and pulsating, thrusting deep inside her as his green eyes locked onto hers.

Norah came as her fantasy melted away and she lay there panting for a few minutes, her body vibrating with the afterglow and her mind whirling. Her orgasm, intense and all-consuming, had made her shiver with desire and longing.

She heard the front door slam, bringing her back to reality. She turned over in the bed, not wanting to talk to Lucian as he stomped up the stairs.

"Norah? You awake?"

She kept her eyes shut, feeling irritated at his presence. God, just leave him already, woman. She stiffened as he got into the bed. He smelled of booze and perfume.

Fucker.

She felt him reach for her and kept her body stiff and unresponsive. "Come on, baby," he slurred, "Wake up for daddy."

She wanted to throw up. He knew she hated it when he got like this—drunk and sloppy—and he did it deliberately. The "daddy" thing had always revolted her and it was a new thing too. Did his other girlfriend like it?

Lucian's hand was between her legs now, and finally, she reacted. "What the hell are you doing?"

He laughed. "Just getting mine. C'mon, honey, we haven't done it for weeks."

She edged away from him, but he grabbed hold of her arm. "Let me go, Lucian."

"You know what? No. You're my girlfriend, dammit ..."

He moved quickly, pulling her back onto the bed and covering her body with his, his hands burrowing. "Get off me," she growled at him, getting more annoyed and scared, but he didn't let her go. His fingers were seeking her sex now.

"Why are you wet? See, ready for me, just like I wanted."

Norah was crying now as he pinned her to the bed. "Lucian, stop, stop ..."

But he didn't stop, thrusting his half-erect cock into her and thrusting his hips as she cried and struggled to get away from him, sobbing her rage and hurt. He kissed her roughly and she bit down on his tongue, hard.

"Fucking bitch!" And he hit her across the face, hard.

The shock of the assault was icy cold and Norah's whole body shut down. Lucian continued his rape, thrusting and grunting until he came. "See, baby? See how much I love you? God," he buried his face in her neck. "Don't ever leave me, Norah. You ever leave me and I'll kill you ...I'll kill you ..."

Frozen, Norah lay under him, and after a few minutes, Lucian was snoring. She shoved him off her. He didn't wake as she slid from the bed. She got dressed, pulling her hold-all from the closet and dumping her clothes and toiletries into it. Downstairs, she attached Ziggy's lead, grabbed her laptop and phone, and got into her car. Without looking back, she drove into the city and straight to Zulika's apartment.

When Zulika opened the door, she was shocked to see Norah's face, wan and pale. Dry-eyed but obviously devastated, Norah let Zulika lead her into the apartment, then said, very calmly, "I need you to take me to the nearest police station, Zul. I have to report a rape."

GIACOMO SMILED at his friends as they sat around the outside dinner table. Ferma was perched on Giacomo's knee, showing him how to draw the perfect spacecraft, and Carmel was leaning against a reasonably drunk Orlando. Lando raised his glass. "To my family, my beautiful wife and daughter, and my brother, Giacomo."

Giacomo buried a grin and Carmel rolled her eyes. "Fourth time tonight, hun."

They had enjoyed sizzling hot fajitas and two or three bottles of red wine, and now it was getting late.

"Come on, fruit bat." Carmel lifted her daughter up. "Time for bed. Give Jack a kiss."

Ferma threw her arms around her godfather's neck and kissed his cheek. Giacomo chuckled. "Night, mio caro."

While they were alone, Lando studied his friend. "You look different. Upbeat."

Giacomo smiled and ran his hand through his dark curls. "And if I told you why ..."

Lando laughed. "Please, make my day and tell me it's a woman."

"It is," Giacomo admitted wryly. "And not the one it's supposed to be."

"I figured. Who is she?"

"Her name is Norah Reddy she's a brilliant graphic designer, and she has a boyfriend. That would beokay—after all, I couldn't date someone who worked for me—except for one thing."

"What's that?"

Giacomo hesitated for a long moment. "I think Norah's boyfriend is the one screwing Tara."

Lando was sober then. "Oh god, Jack ..."

"I know. What a fucking mess." He gave a humorless laugh. "I've been saying that a lot lately."

Lando sighed. "Man ...does she know? I mean, this Norah girl? Does she know?"

"I don't think so."

"Hell."

"Yup."

They sat in silence for a few minutes, then Lando leaned forward. "You like her?"

Giacomo nodded. "Very much. She's ...the opposite of Tara."

"Man, I think it's time you ended things with Tara. You haven't been happy with her for years."

"She asked me the other night why I had never proposed to her. I gave her some guff about not wanting to settle down and hurt her career."

"Did she buy it?"

"No. I think we both know it's over at this point. God, I knew she was cheating and my instinct was to find out who with, but now I wish I never knew. I wish I had just had the guts to finish it."

They sat in silence until Carmel came back down and rejoined them. "Men? Have we moved into serious territory?"

"Jack's got a crush."

Carmel grinned at Giacomo. "How many times have I told you, Jacky? I'm married."

"Sucks, my mistake." He grinned at her, but then his smile faded. "Carmel, I met someone. Someone ...special. But I also know something that could break her heart. Do I tell her?"

Carmel didn't have an answer for him.

CHAPTER FOUR

Zulika took her friend to the police, then accompanied her to the hospital for the rape kit. She saw the burgeoning bruise on Norah's face and her stomach roiled with fury. When she was sure that Norah was asleep, back safe in Zulika's apartment, she called her step-brother. He was still asleep.

"Motherfucker," she hissed down the telephone at him. Lucian was awake then.

"Zul, what the hell is going on?"

In the background, she could hear sirens and she smiled grimly. "Hear those blues and twos, cocksucker? They're coming for you. I saw what you did to her. I saw the bruises on her face. You fucking raped Norah."

"What the fuck? Rape? I had sex with my girlfriend, Zulika, not that it's any of your business ...and where the hell is Norah? Norah!"

She heard him call out for his absent girlfriend and it made her growl. "You don't even remember, do you? You hit her, Lucian, then you forced yourself on her. Rape, dear brother, is rape. God, I could kill you."

"What?" Lucian's voice had changed from confused to scared now. "No ...no ... I couldn't have ...god ..."

Zulika heard the knock at Lucian's door. "Better get that, asshole. It's time for your walk in perp irons. You'll never see her again. Do you understand? Neither of us. Don't come near either of us ever again or I'll have you arrested."

"Zul ...please, call my lawyer ..." She heard the police inside his apartment now, telling him to hang up the phone.

"Go fuck yourself." She said and hung up the phone. Tears began to fall down her cheeks and, trembling, she buried her face in a pillow to muffle her sobs. The shock of what happened was hitting her now, but she knew it was nothing to what Norah must be feeling. Zulika couldn't believe it; she had never liked her step-brother, but had never thought him capable of this.

She felt an arm slip around her shoulders and looked up to see Norah was awake. They hugged each other for a long time.

"Don't cry," Norah said gently, which of course made Zulika cry even harder.

"Why are you comforting me? You've been through hell."

Norah opened her mouth to argue, but her body slumped and she nodded. "I guess it's just hitting me."

Ziggy, his eyes mournful, padded over to the two women and stuck his snout between them. Norah gave a little laugh and hugged him. "The only man I can rely on," she said, stroking his silky head.

They sat up until dawn, talking about what she would do next. "Stay with me," Zulika begged and Norah agreed.

"Just for now," she said and told Zulika about the apartments she had already scouted out. "I was lying to myself for so long, Zul. It's been over for months, maybe even years."

Zulika nodded. "I think we both needed to break up with the asshole. It's not as if our parents are even married anymore."

Norah didn't know what to say about that. "I can't thank you enough for being here for me."

Zulika hugged her again. "You are my family, Norah. It's you and me against the world. You, me, and this fur ball." She scratched Ziggy's ears. "Monday, you start your new job with that gorgeous man."

"God, that seems like a million years ago. Was it really only a few hours?" Norah's thoughts were in a muddle, she was so tired.

Eventually they fell asleep on Zul's bed, Ziggy between them, and slept until mid-afternoon.

LUCIAN DID NOT WANT his father finding out about his arrest, so he called the one person he knew had enough money to bail him out. Tara arrived, steaming angry, in heavy disguise at the station and posted bail. Lucian tried to kiss her and she stopped him.

"Not here," she growled and stalked off, leaving him to trail behind. In her car, speeding out of the city to a motel they often used, she railed against his calling her. "Giacomo could have found out," she hissed at him. "Or the paparazzi. What if they had taken you to the same station as they do all the celebs? The press pays the police to tip them off. If someone recognized me …"

She ranted all the way to the motel. In the room, he realized she hadn't even asked him what he had done to be arrested. He waited until she had finished admonishing him.

"Baby, I'm sorry. It's a big mess anyway."

"What did you do?"

"What they have accused me of," he corrected, "is assault and rape. What happened is very different."

She folded her arms. "So what happened? Who did you allegedly rape?"

Lucian sighed. "Norah. We had sex. I got a little rough and she cried foul."

Tara stared at him. "You told me you two didn't have sex anymore."

"We rarely do. I was drunk and missing you …"

"So it's my fault, is it?"

"I didn't say that. Anyway, we fucked and then she bit me, so I slapped her. Lightly. Playfully."

Tara curled her nose up. "She likes it rough?"

No. Lucian swallowed hard. "Yes," he lied. Tara sat down beside him, and after a moment, brushed her lips against his.

"Fine, you're forgiven. When is your court date?"

Lucian kissed her again. "I don't know yet. Can we talk about something different? Or rather, now that we're here, do something different?"

Tara smiled. "Lie back." Lucian obeyed and she stripped his trousers and underwear from him, taking his cock into her mouth and sucking hard and long until he was rigid and trembling. She pulled her own panties down and straddled him, lowering herself onto his cock and moving her hips along with his. Lucian lost himself in the sensations and slowly his anger, fear, and sadness became numb.

MONDAY MORNING and Norah was beginning to feel like herself again. Well, not really, but at least she had her new job to look forward to. She covered the nasty bruise on her cheek with heavy foundation, which she hated, but made do otherwise with a light coating of mascara on her already thick eyelashes. She slipped into a yellow and orange sundress, which glowed against her dark caramel skin, and some flat pumps. She wanted to be comfortable, but she wanted to look good too—for a good first impression, she grinned to herself. Not for any other reason.

"You look gorgeous." Zulika was approving and Norah flushed.

"Thank you, Zul. God, I'm nervous. Is it natural to be this nervous?"

"Well, when you're going to work for Adonis himself," Zulika grinned at her friend, whose blush deepened even further. "Try not to fuck him on the first day. God, Norah ...I'm sorry. I didn't think," she said when she saw her friend's stricken face, then quickly got up to hug her.

"It's okay." Norah's voice was muffled. "We can't dance around it forever. I need to move past it."

NORAH WAS PUSHING the rape to the back of her mind as she got into her car, but a second later she jumped out of her skin as Lucian knocked on the driver's window.

"Go away," she yelled, locking the doors and windows.

"I just want to talk," Lucian called, holding his hands up. "Look, just open the window an inch so we can hear each other. That's all I ask."

"No. Anything you have to say to me, you can say to my lawyer." She started the car and he backed off.

"Norah ...I'm sorry. That's all I wanted to say. I'm sorry."

Norah watched him turn and walk away from her, getting into his car and driving off. She drew in a deep breath and started the car. The Conti-Tech buildings were out in Mountain View. She would have to drive past her old home.

Tears pricked her eyes then, but she pushed them away. "You don't get to win this, Lucian. You don't get to ruin my big day."

She pulled the car away from the curb and drove towards her new life.

SEB CAME to get her at reception an hour later, grinning and nudging her with his shoulder in a conspiratorial way. Norah was already half-in-love with him and chuckled. "You look more excited than I do," she said. "I'm really not that interesting."

"I beg to differ," Seb said, "I need a new pal around here." He lowered his voice. "All the guys are so straight and so nerdy it's painful. And I told Jack the other day, he's getting old now, so I need a new playmate."

Norah felt her spirits soar only for them to plummet again when Seb continued, "Jack's just having an argument with the dragon at the moment. Sorry, I mean his girlfriend. Hopefully, he's dumping her—we can but hope."

Right on cue, the door opened and a beautiful but icy blonde stalked out. Norah recognized her, but couldn't place her. The blonde met her gaze and they sized each other up. The blonde's eyes narrowed and she stalked out. Seb cheerfully gave the finger to her retreating back.

"Seb," Giacomo was at the door of his office, trying to hide a grin. Seb shrugged good-naturedly.

"Sorry, I have Finger Tourette's. Anyway...here she is!" Seb indicated Norah flamboyantly and Norah burst out laughing. God, how did these two ever get any work done?

Giacomo shook Norah's hand. "Come on in before you're scared off by this lunatic. Sebastiano, can I trust you to field calls for a little while?"

"Take as long as you need," Seb said, a wicked gleam in his eyes. Norah couldn't help but grin at the man. He was fun and she loved that he had already singled her out to be his friend.

And as for the man in front of her ...lord, she would have to try hard not to be distracted by his sensual presence. He was wearing a light blue shirt tucked into dark gray trousers that fit him perfectly. Giacomo smiled at her. "Ready to start work?"

She grinned back at him. Really, his smile was like sunshine. "You bet."

CHAPTER FIVE

By the end of her first week, Norah was flying. It had been intense, exhausting, and high-speed, but she had loved every exhilarating moment of working with Giacomo. He had very fixed thoughts about what he wanted for the campaigns, but he never dismissed her own ideas, listening to them carefully so that in the end, the first draft of the very first advertisement was a fifty-fifty collaboration between them.

More than that, she found him to be great company. He was relaxed, flirtatious without being creepy, and comfortable with himself in a way that Norah envied. But, then again, she supposed that when you looked like Giacomo did, you would be comfortable. It did border on arrogance some of the time, especially when dealing with people she could tell he didn't like, but, never, ever with his employees, or with her.

He came unexpectedly to the Anthology one afternoon when she was working upstairs and she felt shocked at how happy seeing his face made her. *Don't fall for your client, girl.* But she had to admit that she didn't think she could stop herself.

Norah introduced Giacomo—she just couldn't get on board with calling him Jack; it was too generic for a man like him—to

Zulika, who liked him immediately, and to Ziggy who greeted him like an old friend. Norah almost groaned – looks, class, fun, and likes dogs? Yes, please ...

When he invited Norah to come for drinks after a meeting with two of his friends, this time she agreed, and now, as they took a cab into the city, Norah felt nervous—excited nervous, to be sure. Giacomo's arm was across the back of the seat behind her as they rode in the back of the cab. He was chatting easily, but she couldn't help but feel the tension that had been building between them. Giacomo held her gaze as he talked to her, but she barely heard a thing. He seemed to sense the turmoil in her. He stopped talking and let the back of his finger drift down her cheek.

Norah felt her skin vibrating with longing and his warm fingers brushed her collarbone. She closed her eyes, reveling in the feeling of his touch. She felt him move closer, then his lips brushed hers softly. She didn't dare open her eyes. She didn't want to break the spell or have to deal with the fact that she knew this was wrong. He had a girlfriend. He was her client.

His lips were firmer against hers now and she gave a soft moan of desire. His fingers knotted in her long hair and his tongue massaged hers gently. Her hands had a mind of their own, sliding along the length of his hard-muscled thighs.

Norah opened her eyes. Giacomo was gazing at her, his green eyes dark with desire, drinking in every detail of her face. His lips moved against hers so naturally, their breath mingling. Finally, they drew apart and Giacomo smiled ruefully. "I have wanted to do that since we met."

She flushed with pleasure. "Me too ...but, Giacomo, we can't. We work together. You have a girlfriend."

Giacomo nodded sadly. "I know ...and I assume you have a partner at home?"

God, the shock of the reminder sent a pain through her

stomach. Lucian. She shook her head. "No. Not anymore."

Giacomo stroked her hair. "Bella ...we should talk. Not here, obviously," he half-smiled. "But soon. Soon ...I will not have the other ...commitment, and believe me, not just because of the way I am feeling about you. It had been over long before I was aware of your existence. The work thing ...I understand your reticence, but we can work around that. For now, just know ... you are all I think about."

She could hardly breathe. This gorgeous, beautiful, unattainable man wanted her. She knew the truth of it in his gaze, his words, and the tenderness of his touch.

She was still glowing when they reached the bar and she was caught up in the introductions. Orlando and Carmel Price, both strikingly beautiful African-Americans, tall, and with the friendliest smiles, were waiting for her. They introduced themselves to her and teased Giacomo, who clearly adored them.

They ordered drinks and sat in a corner booth. Carmel, a human rights lawyer, chatted to Norah amiably about her work, Norah's work, and Ferma, their daughter. Norah liked the other woman immensely. Orlando was a riot; funny and erudite, his gentle teasing of Norah made her feel at home with them. Giacomo was relaxed, and at one point, Norah noticed him raising his eyebrows at Carmel, who nodded back approvingly. Norah tried not to blush at the obvious sign of approval she was receiving.

THE EVENING WENT ON LONGER than anyone expected and it was only at ten o'clock that Orlando looked ruefully at his watch. "Sorry to say, we have to get back for the sitter. She's probably sitting in the corner, sobbing and rocking back and forth because Ferma's been on a tear."

Norah nearly snorted her drink out of her nose at the image.

"I must meet Ferma. She sounds like my kind of anarchist."

Carmel and Giacomo laughed and Orlando nodded. "She is that. Norah, it has been an absolute delight to meet you and I hope it's just the first of many such evenings."

"Hear, hear," said Carmel as they all stood. She hugged Norah and whispered in her ear. "I shouldn't say this, but Jack's crazy about you."

Norah felt tears prick her eyes. "I like him too," she said, slightly embarrassed, but Carmel grinned at her and squeezed her hand.

"You'll be good for him, sweetie. I can tell."

Orlando gave Norah a bear hug too. "If everyone is free one night next week, can I suggest dinner at our place?"

They agreed on a night, then Carmel and Orlando left them alone. Giacomo held out his hand to her. "Shall we catch a little night air before getting a cab?"

They walked down to the waterfront. Giacomo took her hand and held it, winding his fingers through hers. Norah felt like a giddy teenager and when Giacomo stopped and took her in his arms, she didn't resist. His kiss was intoxicating, soft at first, then as their lips moved together, firmer and rougher until they were both panting. He groaned and broke away. "God, Norah, I'm sorry ...I know this is wrong and, that I should settle things with Tara first, but ..." He looked at her with such tenderness that she wanted to cry. "I want you, Norah ...so badly. In my arms, my bed ...my life. Do you feel it too?"

Norah nodded. "I do." Her voice barely above a whisper, the breath caught in her throat as he came to her again. Leaning his forehead against hers, he met her gaze.

"Come home with me, mio caro ..." The deep timbre of his voice, the accent ...god ...

Norah found herself nodding. "Yes, Giacomo ...yes ..."

. . .

NORAH COULDN'T REMEMBER the cab ride to Giacomo's place. She couldn't remember him leading her into his mansion in Pacific Heights. She couldn't remember him sweeping her off her feet and taking her up the huge staircase to his bedroom. She could remember every moment of what happened next.

Giacomo stripped her slowly, kissing every part of her exposed skin. His hand drifted down under her dress to caress her sex through her panties and she moaned at the touch of him. She cupped the hot, huge length of him through his pants and could feel his desire for her. He murmured her name as her dress fell to the floor and he buried his face in her belly, kissing the soft curve of it, making her shiver in delight. He stood and tugged off his own shirt and pants, and Norah sank to her knees and slid her hands into his underwear, freeing his diamond-hard cock and taking it into her mouth. God, the feel of him. She closed her eyes and licked the salty pre-cum from the sensitive tip. There was no way she could take all of him into her mouth, so she stroked the length of him, tracing a pattern with her tongue on the tip and making him groan her name. She could feel him nearing his peak, then he was pulling her up, ripping her panties from her, laying her on the bed, and plunging his cock deep inside her sodden, wet cunt. Norah wrapped her legs around his hips and arched her back as the sheer pleasure of being fucked by him took her over completely. Giacomo's mouth was on her breasts, taking each nipple into his mouth as his cock plowed deep and long into her.

"God, Giacomo, Giacomo ..." Norah couldn't help but scream his name as his pace increased, his thrusts almost violent, and when he came, she felt the force of his cum shooting deep into her belly. She couldn't take her eyes off him, lost in his intense gaze. They stayed connected as they kissed and panted for breath, then Giacomo slowly moved out of her and lay by her side, gazing down at her.

"Norah, you make me the happiest man," he said, emotion making his voice break. He smoothed his hand down her body. "Beautiful, just beautiful ..."

Norah didn't know how anything else in the world was beautiful besides this man, but her heart warmed at the compliment. She reached down to stroke his cock, as it was already hardening again.

"Giacomo," she nuzzled her nose against his. "You don't know what this means to me, this night ..."

She felt him stroke a finger along her collarbone and knew what he was seeing. A bruise, from Lucian's attack on her.

"What did he do to you, mio caro?" His eyes were dark with danger now. He had obviously guessed she'd been attacked.

"Something unforgivable."

Giacomo nodded, his eyes serious. "I want to kill him for it."

Norah kissed him. "He isn't worth it, Giacomo. He's nothing. What he did to me ...I won't let him ruin my life ...or my sex life. What he did wasn't sex—it was violence. Pure violence."

Giacomo traced the shape of her lip with his finger. "Still, I am surprised you ..."

Norah smiled, a little pang of something inside her. "I know. Me too. If it hadn't been with you, I don't think I could have. Not so soon. But I have to admit ...I've been thinking about this since I met you."

Giacomo grinned, cocky. "Glad to be of service."

Norah laughed, but then her smile faded. "What I don't like is ...now, I have done what I said I'd never do—sleep with another woman's man."

Giacomo kissed her fingers. "Principessa, I am your man. But I do see your point. Believe it or not, I have never been a cheater until now. I have cultivated the image of someone who plays hard and fast with a woman's heart, but I am really not like that."

"Then why do you let people think that?" She was genuinely curious now. He gave her a strange smile.

"Safety net," he said simply and she smiled, her hand stroking his face.

"I understand."

"Somehow I thought you might. I will talk to Tara tomorrow. She's out of town tonight."

"Does she live here?"

Giacomo shook her head. "No, she has her own place. One here and one in New York."

Suddenly Norah didn't want to talk about Tara anymore. She'd already cheated with Giacomo once and now that they had talked ...she pushed him onto his back and straddled him.

He grinned up at her, looking ten years younger, boyish, free, and happy as he stroked her breasts and her belly while she impaled herself on his rock-hard cock. "Bella, the feel of your skin is like silk to me ..."

They made love slowly this time, drinking each other in, then afterward Giacomo took her in the shower, thrusting into her from behind as he held her against the cool tile. Norah felt every inhibition slip away as he fucked her expertly.

She wouldn't stay the night though. "When things are settled with Tara, then I will," she told him, and although he was disappointed, he accepted it. "At least let me drive you home."

The night was warm, so they drove back to Norah's apartment with the top down. Norah enjoyed the feel of the cool air on her skin. Giacomo's hand was on her bare leg as he drove and she smiled over at him.

This whole night has been a dream, she thought, a total dream.

Giacomo kissed her tenderly before he let her go. "Goodnight, mio caro."

. . .

Norah floated back to the apartment. Ziggy gave a delighted woof and padded out of his dog bed to greet her. She sat on the floor with him and hugged him. "My other best man," she murmured, but then nearly jumped out of her skin as Zulika's voice came out of the dark.

"Oh, yes?"

She flicked a lamp on and grinned at a blinking Norah. "You look as if you've been fucked professionally. Can I assume you and the billionaire have been knocking boots?"

Norah flushed scarlet, but couldn't help the smile that crept over her face. "Am I a slut?"

Zulika's eyes widened. "No, but it's true? Yes, yes, yes!" She punched the air triumphantly. "Was he as good as he looks?"

Still burning, Norah sat down next to her friend. "Better."

"Was he huge? He looks huge."

"Zul!"

"Norah?"

Norah chuckled. "Yes, all right? Yes he is …blessed in that department."

"Eggplant or butternut squash?"

"And that's all the detail you're getting," Norah got up, giggling, but Zulika pulled her back down.

"Okay, no more details except …are you okay? I mean, after what happened, I'm surprised that you, you know." Zulika's eyes were concerned, serious now.

Norah hugged her. "Me too, actually. But I'm not letting Lucian destroy my life. I wanted Giacomo, so I had him. Now,= that does sound slutty." She burst out laughing and Zulika joined her.

"No, it doesn't. You know what it sounds like, No-No?"

Norah shook her head. "What?"

Zulika smiled. "Happiness."

CHAPTER SIX

Giacomo asked Tara to meet him at her favorite restaurant. After he'd told her, gently, that it was over between them, she stared at him. "And you thought you'd tell me in public so I wouldn't make a scene?"

Giacomo sighed. "Yes. Is that what you want to hear, Tara? Honesty? Then, yes."

Tara looked away from him and he was surprised to see tears glinting in her eyes. "Tara?"

"I need a smoke. Come outside with me."

They sat on the patio and Tara offered him one of her cigarettes before lighting her own. Giacomo, not trusting this calm, shook his head.

"Tara ...we haven't been happy in god knows how long. You know this."

Tara blew a lungful of smoke out. "I know. I just ...hoped we could find our way back to each other."

Giacomo toyed with the stem of his wine glass. "Tara, I know about Lucian Hargity."

She laughed derisively. "I figured. Lucian means nothing to me."

"And yet he was worth cheating on me with?"

Tara gave him a withering look. "Please, don't tell me you've been entirely faithful to me this all time."

"Until I knew it was over, I was."

She looked skeptical. "Is that why you hired Lucian's girlfriend?"

"Ex-girlfriend, and no. I hired her because she was the best person for the job."

Tara's eyes searched his face. "You've fucked her, haven't you?"

Giacomo said nothing, kept his face blank, and didn't look away from Tara's gaze. Tara made a disgusted noise. "Well, little Miss Pure ain't so pure after all."

That got him. "You don't know the first thing about Norah, so shut your mouth about her."

Tara smirked and Giacomo knew he'd lost that round. He sighed. "Look, Tara, there's no reason this has to be unpleasant. I'm going to go now. Take care of yourself."

Tara watched him walk away from her. God, he was still so attractive to her, even after she'd cheated on him. At the same time ...how dare the fucker dump her? Tara Hubert wasn't dumped. She was never dumped. Who the hell did Giacomo Conti think he was? One thing she did know—she would make him pay for this.

She smiled to herself. "No, Giacomo, you're wrong. There's every reason this has to be unpleasant," she murmured to herself, throwing back the last of her wine. "And it's about to get really fucking unpleasant."

. . .

Norah drove out to Mountain View the next morning, her heart thumping, almost giddy at the thought of seeing Giacomo. Sebastien noticed the change in her as soon as he saw her.

"What have you been up to?" He tried to get it out of her, but Norah, giggling, wouldn't tell. He guessed, of course, as soon as Giacomo walked in, his eyes immediately going to Norah. His smile split his face and Norah flushed bright red. Sebastien sniggered, nudged Norah, then disappeared as his boss glared at him. Giacomo took Norah's hand.

"Come up to my office, Bella."

As soon as the door was closed behind them, he took her in his arms and kissed her. His kiss was so passionate, and so tender that Norah's head spun. Breaking away for air, they smiled at each other.

"I am a single man," he said simply, and she could have cried with happiness when he added, "bBut I hope not to be in the next few minutes. Beautiful Norah, will you be mine?"

"Yes, god, yes." As he reached behind her and locked the door, she was already reaching for his fly. He slid his hands under her skirt, pulling her panties down as she freed his cock, already huge and engorged, from his pants. He lifted her up, bracing her against the wall, and thrust into her.

"God, Principessa, I have been thinking about this all night. The taste of you and your warm, wet cunt wrapped around my cock ..."

Norah kissed him fiercely, wildly turned on by his dirty talk. "Fuck me hard, Giacomo ..."

And he did, making her come over and over, muffling her cries with his mouth. He came explosively, pumping his seed deep inside her.

They didn't get much work done that day, and later, Giacomo took her back to his house and they started over, fucking each other in every different position they could think of. Giacomo moved a mirror so that they could watch themselves screwing, entranced by the sight of his thick, long cock sliding in and out of her red, swollen cunt.

Norah had never known a night like this—wild and uninhibited—he made her feel like a goddess. She had never felt so feminine, or sexy, or so loved. When Giacomo took her from behind, pushing into her ass, she found new realms of pleasure. When he went down on her, she came again and again.

Finally, exhausted and sated, they fell asleep in each other's arms and Norah already knew she was lost.

She was in love with him.

TARA LAY BACK in her bed and studied Lucian as he got dressed. After an unsatisfactory fuck—her words to him—he was annoyed with her. Tara lit a cigarette.

"What's she like?"

"Who?"

"Your ex. The bookseller. Your rape victim."

Lucian shot her a warning look. "That's not funny."

Tara shrugged. "Neither is rape. Anyway, tell me. What is she like?"

Lucian sighed. "What does it matter?"

Tara smiled cruelly. "I just want to know who my ex is fucking."

Lucian stopped. "What?"

Tara stubbed out her cigarette and was studying her own breasts. "He's fucking her. I thought you should know."

Lucian made a disgusted noise. "If you think that, then you're crazy. Norah doesn't sleep around."

Tara's mouth set in a thin smile. "Have you seen Giacomo? The man is a god. He could get a Mary Knoll nun into bed."

Lucian stared at her. "You're serious."

"Deadly."

Tara watched as a myriad of emotions played out across Lucian's face, then he shrugged, feigning nonchalance. "None of my business anymore."

"He knows about you and me."

"I thought you said there was no way."

"Carmel Price must have told him. She never liked me, the stuck-up bitch."

"I thought you said you were taking care of that too."

Tara's smile returned. "Oh, believe me, she won't get away with it."

"Too late now."

"For you and me? Yes."

Lucian stood and tucked his shirt in. "What do you mean?"

Tara waved her hand around vaguely. "I mean this. Us. Thanks for everything and all that, but this is goodbye."

Lucian shook his head. This was nothing new from Tara. "You're a fucking bitch, you know that?"

"As a matter of fact, I do." She laughed suddenly. "Okay then, Lu-lu, I'll give us one last chance. Who knows? We may be made for each other."

As Lucian left the apartment, his gut began to churn with the thought of Norah in bed with another man. And Giacomo Conti ...god ...

He had to get back with Norah ...but how? Part of his bail conditions meant he couldn't go anywhere near her. He needed to get to her via Zulika—which would be a problem because his half-sister hated him even more than Norah did. Still ...Lucian was nothing if not a good actor. Turn on the waterworks. Beg for forgiveness.

Wait for the billionaire to screw someone else, and if he

didn't, if he was truly enamored with Norah, there was no reason that Norah couldn't be made to believe that he had cheated on her.

Lucian began to smile. Norah had been his, and he had been dumb enough to throw it away.

He wouldn't make the same mistake twice.

Lucian called Zulika a few days later, begging her to meet with him, crying down the phone. She had never liked her brother much, but even her cynical heart was touched by his grief.

"I'll meet you," she told him in a firm voice. "But I tell you now, I am one-hundred percent Team Norah. Do you understand?"

"I do." And he sounded genuine. "Just meet with me and hear what I have to say. If you don't like what you hear, fine. Please, Zul."

She met him at a coffeehouse, well away from their apartment or the bookstore. He smiled at her, but she didn't return it—just nodded. "I only have a half hour," she said shortly.

"Just hear me out. That's all I ask."

"Go ahead."

Lucian sighed. "What I did to Norah …it's unforgivable. It was a dumb mistake. No, not a mistake. It was horrendous what I put her through and I take full responsibility for it. I'll go to the D.A. right now and plead guilty if she'll just meet me to talk it through. I don't want her forgiveness. Just …to talk."

Zulika was studying him through narrowed eyes. "Rape, Lucian. You raped her."

"Yes."

There was a long silence. "I never thought you capable of that."

He gave her a half-smile. "Believe me, I had no idea I was. I was just ...I don't know. An animal. A disgusting animal. I'm in AA now. Not that it excuses anything, but it's a start."

"Why should Norah give you the time of day?"

"No reason ...except history. The fact that, because of you, we will always be connected somehow."

Wrong tack. Zulika's face hardened. "I have no problem cutting you out of my life, Lucian. It's not like we have ever been close."

He nodded slowly. "I know. But the thought of losing you both ...it's killing me. I will do my time for what I did to Norah, I swear. I will make this right. Believe it or not, I love both of you."

Zulika sighed. "Okay, let's cut to the chase. Norah is okay. Just okay. That girl has given you more chances than you deserve and she'll probably do it again. So, if you want to make nice, it would create a better atmosphere for everyone. Norah, me, and your Dad. I still think you need to maintain a distance, but hey, that's me. I will tell you this—if she says no, she says no. Don't forget the restraining order is still in effect."

Lucian rolled his eyes. "How could I forget?" He sighed and ran his hands through his hair so it stuck up. "Thing is, I know it's over with Norah. How I thought we could ever make it work—I blew it when I slept with someone else, when I hurt Norah. I'm not stupid. I know that part of it is over. But I miss my buddy, my pal. We had a few great years together."

She nodded. "If you think you can be just friends, then God be with you."

"I'd like to try."

Zulika chewed her lip. "I don't know what Norah will say. I'll talk to her, but I'm not going to plead your case—just repeat verbatim what you've said here today. Do you understand that?"

Lucian nodded. "I do."

They sat in silence for a few minutes while Zulika contemplated her step-brother. She sat up and nodded at him. "Okay, tell you what. I'll talk to Norah for you. I will." She hesitated before continuing. "I'm going to tell you something else, and how you react to it will tell me for sure if I'm crazy for trusting you, okay?"

She waited for him to process what she'd said. She could see the myriad of questions whirling around his head. Finally, he nodded.

Zulika took a deep breath and hoped she wasn't about to make the biggest mistake of her life.

GIACOMO TRAILED his fingers down the length of her spine as Norah bent over her design table. She shivered with pleasure, then chuckled. "You're distracting me, Conti. I'm trying to sketch here."

"This sundress has no back. How do you expect me to concentrate on anything but your honey skin?" He pressed his lips to her spine and she gave up, laughing.

"We will never get this job finished at this rate." She turned and smiled at him.

"I don't care." He bent his head to kiss her. The last month had been the happiest of her life, Working with Giacomo during the day and making love with him all night. Her life had changed so rapidly that it made her head spin.

She had spent time with him and his friends, and –Zulika— who was once again between boyfriends and so was co-opted by Sebastien as his new buddy—and found her life enriched by all of their presence. The only dark cloud was Lucian. Zulika had come to her and reported what he had said, but Norah shook her head. "No. I'm sorry. I can't."

She had told her lawyer she would drop the charges on the condition that Lucian never came near her again and that she got full and final custody of Ziggy. She didn't want the court case and she most definitely didn't want her new relationship brought into the spotlight. Lucian had agreed and now she had a lifelong restraining order and her freedom.

Giacomo noticed her reverie. "Penny for them?"

"Nothing," she smiled, "Just taking pause, reflecting on my life. I have never been happier, baby."

He grinned. "You know what we need? A vacation."

She grinned. "Damn, boy, you will do just about anything to get out of work, won't you?"

He laughed. "Fine. I'll ask you again, later, when my cock is buried deep inside your delicious cunt ...I find you agree to most things then."

She broke into laughter. "Such a dirty boy ...but," she grinned wickedly, glancing over at his office door, which was shut but not locked, then slowly pulling up her skirt, "Why wait until later?"

Giacomo grinned and made to walk to the door, but she stopped him, a sly grin on her face. "No. Leave it."

His eyes widened for just a second, then he moved, quick as a cat, his hands under her dress, tearing her panties from her. Norah gasped in excitement as he hitched her legs around his waist, unzipping his fly to release his cock, then thrusting into her. He pinned her hands down on the sloping desk and fucked her hard and fast, his eyes never leaving hers. She came just as they heard voices in the ante-office and he muffled his groan as he came inside her.

A knock at the door. "Just a moment, please." Giacomo pulled out and they both, breathless and laughing, tidied themselves up. Norah bent back over her work, trying not to giggle as Giacomo strode to the door.

Sebastian—whoe clearly knew exactly what had gone on—was grinning wildly. "Just wanted to tell you that catering has arrived."

Giacomo kept his face straight. "Thanks, Seb."

"No problem," he called over his shoulder. "By the way, I think it's hot –dogs—unless you've just had one, Norah ..." He cackled with laughter.

"Thank you, Seb." Giacomo could barely hold it together then and Norah let a giggle out, then couldn't stop until she was crying with laughter. Giacomo was shaking his head, grinning.

"I'm going to fire that guy."

Norah put her arms around his neck. "Don't you dare." She kissed him. "Or I won't come on vacation with you."

"You'll let me take you away?"

She grinned. "I will. After we've finished this campaign."

"Tyrant."

"Hot dog."

CHAPTER SEVEN

Carmel was absolutely sure she was being followed now, and with Orlando, she went to the police. The officer who dealt with them was kind, but told them unless they could gather some actual evidence to prove she was being followed, there was little they could do.

"I thought California had pretty stringent stalking laws now?" Orlando asked, his expression wan and concerned. The officer, Det. Lawrence, nodded.

"But until we can prove definitively that Mrs. Price is being stalked by someone, and who that someone might be, we can't do anything. Your work as a human rights lawyer, Mrs. Price, may, of course, throw some light on who would be a suspect. Could you make a list?"

"Of course."

They thanked him for his time and he promised that he would follow up with them.

They went for coffee afterward at a small diner they knew. Orlando was distracted and Carmel tried to cheer him up. "Sweetie, look, maybe it's nothing."

"And maybe it's something."

She touched his face. They had been married for nine years now, and every day they spent with each other just strengthened their bond. They had met in college and they both bemoaned the cliché, but to hell with it, that's where she had fallen in love with the tall, rangy musician. With her focus on law, they couldn't have been more different with their passions, but they became inseparable from the first day, when, after a boozy evening in the student bar, they discovered they shared the same sarcastic, dry humor and were equally as disdainful of the pretentious arty set. They had enough in common to have something to talk about and enough differences to make it interesting. He'd had competition, of course. Almost every man at the college, including the tutors, practically drooled when they saw her, but to her credit, she was completely oblivious to the attention.

Orlando won her precisely because he made an effort to see past the dark Creole good looks inherited from her mother. To him, she revealed a humorous, intelligent side and confidence tempered with humility. And in turn, she brought him out of his shell. He was still shy, but hid it well, the result being that people would often find him the life of the party. If only they knew the real man. When he'd come to California from Oregon at fifteen, he'd felt like a shadow—half a person. His beloved Aunt Kathleen, who'd raised him from a boy, had been an amateur photographer and her enthusiasm and vision had inspired him. He'd applied to the art college. Orlando strongly believed in fate and when, on the first day of college, he saw the lovely, dark girl full of life and laughter bounding through the corridors, something had changed over in him and he measured the start of his life from that moment.

"Baby," she said now and smiled at him, bringing him back into the present. "I say we change the subject. I've been thinking. Now that Ferma is getting so big …maybe she'd like a sibling."

Orlando looked surprised. "What happened to, 'Impregnate me again, and I'll feed your danglers to a rabid dog?'"

Carmel laughed. "You can't hold me to comments I made in the middle of a fifteen-hour labor."

"The image was so striking, it haunts me. But he grinned and took her hand. "You want another anarchist?"

She nodded. "I do. I'm really ready."

Orlando leaned across the table and kissed her. "Then I am too. Let's do it."

Norah kept her word and as soon as the campaign finished, Giacomo flew them down to his private island in the Caribbean. Walking through the airy, spacious villa, Norah marveled at the beauty of it all. Giacomo showed her around the property—beach-front, palm-trees with their silky, spiky fronds hanging down, and the crystal clear blue ocean.

Norah couldn't quite take it all in. "It's unreal ..." The villa itself had huge glass sliding doors on almost every wall, even in the bedroom. Giacomo smiled at her raised eyebrows. "The perks of being the only ones here," he said. "At least at night."

He slid his arms around her. "I can fuck you all night long with the windows wide open and no-one would hear your cries as I make you come again ...and again ...and again ..."

She moaned as he trailed his lips across her cheek and fixed them onto her mouth. It was a matter of seconds before he had tumbled her to the cool tile floor and spread her legs. "What do you taste like today, beautiful?" He grinned before his mouth found her sex, his teeth grazing her clit before he lashed his tongue around it. Norah shivered and closed her eyes, losing herself in the sensations as his tongue dipped inside her. Then she felt him slip two fingers inside of her and begin to rub as he sucked at her clit, nipping it gently between his teeth. Norah moaned and writhed as she became unbearably aroused and her back arched up as she came, hard and long. Giacomo moved swiftly, plunging his cock into her as she was still coming, and she almost screamed at the sensation of his huge, thick cock filling her.

"I'm going to nail you to the floor, Principessa," he growled and began to fuck her hard, thrusting with intense, long movements and watching her expression as Norah, half-crazed, orgasmed again and again.

When his own moment came, he pulled out and ejaculated onto the soft skin of her belly. Norah smiled, her fingernails digging into his thighs as he pumped the thick, hot semen onto her. "God, you make me crazy," he groaned, "Norah ...ti amo ...ti amo ..."

Tears began to drop down Norah's face from the sheer passion in his voice. "I love you too," she whispered. "Giacomo, so, so much ..."

She couldn't imagine ever being anywhere but here, now, in this moment, and as they made love long into the night, neither could imagine life with the other.

BUT OF COURSE, fairytales always, always end ...

TWO WEEKS LATER, Norah opened the Anthology early, still energized from her vacation. She and Giacomo had professed their love for each other again and again in their holiday idyll, and now she had some major news to share with Zulika.

Zulika, her blue eyes crinkling with smiles, greeted her a half hour later. "Hey, you,. You look amazing. That man is better than any makeup."

Norah laughed. "No arguments here." She bent down to hug Ziggy. "How's my big boy?"

Zulika stuck her tongue in her cheek. "So many jokes, so

little time," she quipped, then went to the door as a delivery van pulled up. "Uh-oh, I think this one's for you."

A man bearing an enormous bouquet of exotic flowers came staggering into the bookstore. "Miss Reddy? For you."

Between them, Norah and Zulika wrestled the bouquet onto a table and thanked the delivery driver. "Don't need to ask who they're from." Zulika buried her nose in them. "God, heavenly. I take it these are all native to your island?"

Norah, smiling, nodded. "I saw them all there. God, how lovely."

Zulika fished the card out and handed it to her. Norah opened it.

I love you. That is all.

Yours always,

G. x

(p.s. the hibiscus reminds me of something...)

Norah giggled and the card to Zulika, who rolled her eyes. "You two are like a full-on porn movie."

Norah shrugged. "Pretty much." She snagged her phone from her purse. "How very Georgia O'Keefe of you," she read aloud as she wrote a text message to Giacomo, "Thank you for the beautiful flowers ...come play with my hibiscus anytime. I love you."

Zulika cackled with laughter. "Seriously, No-No, that man has unleashed your inner slore."

Norah pretended to be affronted. "Excuse me, I happen to be a strumpet."

"A harlot."

"A lady of disrepute."

"A trollop."

That made them both giggle so much that they couldn't speak for a while. Zulika wiped her eyes and Norah cleared her throat.

"Actually, I do have some other news."

Zulika's eyes immediately dropped to Norah's flat stomach and Norah grinned. "Slow your roll there, cowboy. I'm just moving in with Giacomo is all."

Zulika squealed and hugged her. "Seriously, Norah ...I'm so happy for you."

Norah hugged her. "Thank you, baby. Now, let's get some work done."

G<small>IACOMO</small>, of course, couldn't stay away long. He arrived at lunchtime and bore Norah off to a little trattoria in the city. They shared a plate of pasta and half a bottle of a superb white wine, chatting easily and enjoying the warm day.

It wasn't until Giacomo was paying the check that Norah saw her. Tara. Norah had learned enough about the blonde woman now that she recognized her immediately as she walked towards Norah. Norah didn't like the smile on her face.

"You must be Norah."

Norah gazed back at Tara coolly. "You must be Tara."

Tara smirked and sat down without being asked. Norah glanced at Giacomo, who was talking to the maître d" and hadn't seen them. "What do you want?" She asked Tara, who lit a cigarette and observed her for a few moments.

"Just wanted to see my replacement. He's a good fuck, isn't he?" She flicked the ash of her cigarette and didn't wait for a reply. "Lovely, thick cock and he knows how to use it. And that face ..."

Norah's expression hardened. "I'll ask again, in case you're stupid enough not to understand my question. What do you want?"

Tara cackled. "Oh, you have some fire in your belly. Good.

That's good. You'll need that when he screws around on you. And he will screw around on you, Norah, mark my word."

"Please leave."

Tara didn't move. "You know why he's with you, of course. I'll tell you, unless you're under the illusion that you have some sort of magical cunt that he can't resist. Payback."

Norah sighed. "I really don't care what you think."

Tara's mouthed formed into a perfect O. "You really don't know, do you?"

Giacomo was there then, his face full of anger. "Tara, what the fuck are you doing here?"

She smirked, completely unfazed by his annoyance. "Just filling in your lovely whore on the real reason you're fucking her."

She turned back to Norah. "He knew, you know."

"Tara, shut your damn mouth." Norah had never seen Giacomo look so angry. She stood and took his arm, her eyes cold as she looked at the blonde woman.

"I really don't care what you have to say."

She began to walk away when Tara called after her. "Lucian. Giacomo knew I was screwing him before he offered you a job. Before he fucked you. That's what I mean by payback. It was revenge, you stupid bitch."

Norah felt her heart stop. She looked up at Giacomo, who shook his head. "That had nothing to do with ..."

"You knew. You knew your girlfriend was screwing my boyfriend ...and then, what? Giacomo?"

"It had nothing to do with the way I feel about you, mio caro. Nothing. I love you."

Norah pulled her arm away from him. "But you knew ...and you never told me?"

Giacomo closed his eyes. "Norah ..."

"You bastard." She whispered the words, her voice breaking. She heard Tara behind her.

"He's just like all of the rest of them. Just like Lucian."

A fury rose up in Norah and she turned and slapped Tara's face, hard. Tara, laughing, staggered, but righted herself as Norah, with burning anger and hurt in her eyes, looked at Giacomo.

"You're a liar and a user. Go find someone else to play your twisted games with."

Giacomo reached out for her, but she ducked out of his reach. "Don't follow me."

Tears pouring down her face, she fled down the street, hailing the nearest cab. Giacomo had arranged this all. She was a mere pawn in his and Tara's twisted game.

Her chest felt like it was being ripped open and she bent double, trying to drag air into her lungs. The cab driver cast worried looks in the mirror. "Hey, now, are youokay? Do you need to hurl?"

"No, I'm okay. Just, please, get there fast."

At Zulika's apartment, she barely made it into the room before collapsing to the floor and sobbing her heart out. Zulika, terrified, couldn't get a coherent answer out of her. Instead she managed to wrestle her into her bedroom and put her to bed, encouraging Ziggy to lay next to his weeping mistress.

GIACOMO TURNED up at the apartment an hour later, but Zulika wouldn't let him in. "Giacomo, no. She doesn't want to see you."

He looked devastated. "Please, Zul. I need to explain what really happened to her."

Zulika felt like she had been refereeing her best friend's love life for months now. "Just give her some time."

He had agreed, but Zulika could see the pain in his eyes and knew he was genuine. "I love her. Please just tell her that."

"I will," she whispered before closing the door.

Norah was in her room, knees hugged to her chest. "Was that him?" Zulika couldn't stand to hear the break in her voice.

"Yes, honey." She sat down and stroked her friend's hair. "He's a mess."

"He lied to me. He used me."

Zulika didn't know what to say. She understood why Norah was reacting this way; at the same time, she thought this was more about Norah's fragile trust being broken than what Giacomo had done. Zulika didn't believe for a moment that Giacomo had seduced Norah out of a need for revenge. But since the rape, she didn't think Norah had processed her feelings, instead blanketing it out with her affair with Giacomo. Maybe she did need some space to reflect and heal.

CHAPTER EIGHT

It had been a week since the row, and Giacomo, desperate as he was, had managed to stay away. Now, though, he couldn't wait any longer.

As Giacomo walked into the bookstore, Norah looked up. Zulika greeted him warily.

"Hey, Zul." He half-smiled at her and looked over to Norah. She looked away and went out into the back room, closing the door behind her. Giacomo sighed.

"Give her time," Zulika said in a low voice. He nodded, his eyes heavy and sad.

"Do you want some coffee?"

He hesitated, looking back at the closed door. He shook his head. "No, I ..." His voice broke and he turned and walked out. Head down, he strode across the road, clearing his throat and trying to relieve some of the tension and misery. He got into his car and headed for Orlando's home. He needed someone to talk to now; Sebastien, usually his sounding board, was annoyed with him. Rightly so, Giacomo thought now, how could I have been so stupid?

He couldn't shake the feeling that he'd lost her forever and the thought made him want to scream and scream and never stop.

Zulika let herself into the back room, knocking lightly on the door. She saw Norah, dry-eyed now, cleaning the tile floor with harsh, angry movements. She didn't look at Zulika.

"You okay?"

Norah didn't answer her. Zulika saw the tearstains dried on her face and the red of her eyes.

"Honey ...you should give him a break."

Norah looked at her with a hard expression. "Should I?"

Zulika nodded, trying to smile at her. "He's devastated. Truly. He's hurting. Badly, Norah. Really badly."

"Really?"

Zulika nodded. "You know he is."

Norah's jaw clenched. "And yet somehow it's me who gets screwed once again because a man can't keep it in his pants. How ironic."

Zulika looked down. Norah slammed down the mop on the floor, scrubbing the mess away.

"He didn't sleep with you to get revenge. I think you know that. Giacomo Conti is a man in love. With you, Norah."

Norah stopped. "Don't. Don't defend him. It's too late for that."

Zulika looked her straight in the eye. "It shouldn't be. This isn't about Giacomo and I think you know that."

Norah gave a humorless laugh. "So what's it about?"

"You were raped, Norah. That's what this is about."

"Don't."

"You know it is, darling. You're just using this as an excuse. You know in your heart that Giacomo Conti is in love with you

—and you're pushing him away because, deep down, you think you're damaged goods."

Something in Zulika's voice broke through Norah's anger. She stopped mopping, her expression pained and haunted, and she stared at Zulika for a long moment.

"You think I haven't processed the rape."

Zulika shook her head. "No."

Norah looked away, all her anger disappearing. She sat down on the couch and dropped her head into her hands. "You don't think Giacomo used me?"

"No."

Norah closed her eyes. "But then why the hell didn't he tell me?"

Zulika went over to her friend and tried to smile at her. "He did try. You should give him a second chance, honey—and you should definitely get some therapy."

Norah half-smiled. "I'm so tired, Zulika. Maybe I need some time alone."

Zulika hugged her. "Do you really want to be away from him?"

Norah sighed and leaned into her friend. "I don't, but maybe I should just take pause."

"You do what you think is right."

"I will. I promise. I need some time for me, I think."

Zulika smiled, trying to lighten the mood. "You've been doing those incantations again, haven't you?" She grabbed her friend and stared hard at her, her eyes crinkling. "Repeat after me: I am a strong independent woman. I am a strong independent woman. Who really, really, wants to give her best friend a colossal and completely undeserved pay bump."

Norah laughed then and hugged her. "It wouldn't be undeserved."

Zulika's eyes lit up. "Then I get a pay bump?"

Norah smiled. "I didn't say that. Come on, let's get to work. I could use the distraction."

Giacomo was in such a mess that Orlando persuaded him to stay with them for the weekend. They got a sitter for Ferma on a Saturday night and took him to their favorite bar, Fonseca's.

He was hollow-cheeked and his eyes were haunted as he told them how Tara had "reached out" to him. "She destroys my life, then tries to worm her way back in. Unbelievable." He shook his head and Orlando and Carmel exchanged a glance.

"Tara is nothing but a waste of space," Carmel said. "Don't waste any time thinking about her. You said Zulika was on your team?"

Giacomo half-smiled. "It's the only thing giving me hope."

Orlando felt for his friend. He and Carmel had sat up nights talking about the situation, hurting for their best friend. They had been distracted from their own lives and had been amazed when Carmel fell pregnant almost immediately after they'd made the decision to try. They hadn't told anyone yet, not even Ferma, and they kept their joy between them, especially in the face of Giacomo's sadness.

Now Carmel reached over and squeezed her friend's hand. "I know in my heart that she'll come back to you, Jacky. I've never seen two people more in love—apart from Lando and me, of course," she added hurriedly, grinning at her husband, and they were both gratified to see Giacomo half-smile.

"If Norah and I were ever as happy as you two, it would be a dream come true."

"Don't give up on that dream, buddy."

TARA WAS chain-smoking one cigarette after another. She had thought Giacomo would be angry with her, but the fury in him after she'd spoken to Norah that day was like nothing she had ever experienced. She'd chosen the wrong play. She knew that now, but still ...Giacomo's anger had scared her. He was clearly deeply in love with Lucian's ex-girlfriend, and seeing Norah up close, Tara saw the beauty of the young woman. Her friendliness, and warmth ate away at her. She had everything that Tara wanted; everything that Tara once had and was desperate to regain. Joy. Beauty. Giacomo.

So, that hadn't worked, but Tara knew exactly how to bring her former lover to his knees and she was looking forward to seeing Giacomo Conti utterly destroyed.

She pulled out her phone and dialed. "They're at Fonseca's. You know what to do."

She ended the call and started the car, pulling away from the sidewalk outside the bar. Tonight, it begins, Giacomo. Tonight.

CARMEL EXCUSED herself to use the bathroom. She sighed to herself. Damn you, Tara, for making my friend so miserable. Giacomo was as devastated as she'd ever seen him. Carmel knew that he and Norah would have been good together. Maybe she would call the other woman to try and help mend things. She knew what Lando would say—don't interfere. But she couldn't stand by while two people who were as crazy about each other as Giacomo and Norah tore themselves apart.

She used the bathroom and was washing her hands when she heard the bathroom door click locked. She looked up to see a man entirely dressed in black, his face covered, and in his hand, a gun leveled at her. Her blood froze. No, this can't be happening ...

She backed away from him as he moved toward her. "What the hell are you doing? Who are you?" She thought she had asked him out loud, but realized the silence of the bathroom had been broken by neither of them, and when she saw a long silencer attached to the front of the gun, Carmel could barely breathe.

"Please ...I'm pregnant ...and I have a daughter, a seven-year-old-daughter ..."

The first bullet hit her in the stomach. Carmel doubled up, the force of the shot taking her breath away. The second bullet tore through her shoulder, smashing her collarbone. She slumped to the floor, the pain taking over. Her killer calmly walked up to her and crouched beside her. Carmel tried to see his eyes. "Please ...don't ..."

He pressed the muzzle against her belly and emptied the rest of the gun into her.

ORLANDO ENDED the call as Giacomo returned with the drinks. His friend looked around. "Where's Carmel?"

"Bathroom," Orlando said, then checked his watch, frowning. "Maybe she got lost." He stood and looked over the crowded room. "I'll just go check to see she's okay."

His heart was pounding as he approached the hotel bathrooms and when he heard the scream he started to run. A young blonde girl came out of the ladies' bathroom screaming, and instantly Orlando knew. He grabbed the young girl. "What is it?"

"I think she's dead," the young blonde sobbed. "There's so much blood."

He burst into the bathroom, but then was stopped. It felt like a hammer blow. Carmel was propped in a sitting position against the far wall in a pool of her blood. He could tell instantly that she had been shot, her hand on her belly uselessly trying to stem the flow of blood. He darted to her side, his heart hammering, his fingers pressing against her neck trying to find a pulse.

"Oh, my god." Giacomo's shocked voice behind him. "Call 911. Now!" He barked the instruction at a shocked-looking bartender who scurried off. Giacomo approached Orlando, who was cradling Carmel in his arms. "Carmel?"

"I can't find a pulse." Orlando's voice was haunting. His hand was pressed against her wounds, her head on his shoulder. "Please don't leave me, Carmel. Please....not now, not like this ..."

As Giacomo watched, his friend broke down, sobbing over the brutalized body of the woman he loved, begging her to live ...

THE ASSASSIN REPORTED BACK to his client, who thanked him warmly. She chuckled. "I wish I could have seen Giacomo's face ...listen. I may need you again in the future if my plan doesn't work out. I may need you to kill someone else for me. Another woman. I'll send you the details, but I don't want anything to happen to her yet. Just watch her for now."

The killer nodded. "And the name?"

Tara Hubert smiled. "Her name is Norah Reddy and when I give the order, I want you to make that bitch suffer before she dies ..."

HIS LIPS TRAILED across her collarbone as he slowly entered her, his cock huge and throbbing as he pushed inside of her. Norah gasped, tightening her legs around his waist, and pulling his lips up to meet hers. "I love you, Giacomo."

His eyes were intense on hers as he nodded, his skin on hers, thrusting harder and deeper with every stroke. "Ti amo, Norah, ti amo ..."

NORAH STOOD UNDER THE SHOWER, thinking of the dream. It felt so sensory, so real—Giacomo's hands on her body, his mouth on hers, his breath mixing with hers. Norah shook herself. He lied and used you for revenge, she told herself. It doesn't matter how gorgeous he is, how much fun you had together, or how much you ache for him. He's a liar. He'd broken all his promises, destroyed her trust, and hurt her heart. She swallowed the lump in her throat. She raised her face to the spray to clear the tears that suddenly dripped down her face. Focus on something else. Tara Hubert. Even now, the image of Tara's triumphant face was clear in her mind. Norah smiled grimly. A part of her, she was ashamed to admit to herself, plotted Tara's downfall. She could go to the press about the whole affair. After all, she didn't owe anything to Tara and Lucian—nor Giacomo. Norah indulged the fantasy for a second but knew she would do no such thing. Don't stoop to her level, she told herself. Prove I'm not like her. She finished rinsing the conditioner from her hair and stepped out from the shower.

Fall was setting in over San Francisco and a cool breeze drifted through her window as she dressed and dried her hair. Zulika had gone to the bookshop, taking Ziggy with her, and Norah had the day off. A day off to brood and stew, she thought. She decided to distract herself with some mindless television while she baked a cake for Zulika. She flicked on the television, only half listening to the banal chitchat of the morning anchors as she put together the ingredients for an angel food cake. The local news station interrupted as she was scraping the mixture out of the bowl into the baking tin. Norah heard the name and the blood in her veins froze.

This just in: Prominent San Francisco human rights lawyer, Carmel Price, was shot to death last night in the bathroom of a downtown bar. The Harvard law graduate was married with a young child. Police are searching for the gunman, who evaded the club's security cameras, and say that the lawyer's recent international courtroom battles may have something to do with the killing.

Her head whirled and she gripped the counter for support, suddenly breathless. She sank to the floor, breathing in great gulps of air and trying to clear her head. She moved her head and her ears buzzed. Her skin suddenly felt as if a thousand fire ants had stung her. She crawled across the floor to the television.

"No ...no ..." Norah couldn't breathe as a photo of Carmel was flashed up, followed by a video of a distraught-looking Orlando carrying a sobbing Ferma. Behind them, Giacomo, his face contorted with anger and despair, cursed and pushed away the thronging paparazzi as all three of them made their way from the hospital entrance to Giacomo's limousine. Norah's breath was coming in short, panicked sobs now, and unthinkingly, she left everything as it was, grabbed her car keys, and ran from the apartment.

She barely registered where she was going until she pulled onto Orlando's street and slammed on her brakes. What the hell was she doing?

She shook herself. Should she have come? She realized tears were pouring down her cheeks and inside her there was a need, a desperation to reach out and comfort her friends...

You've only known them for such a short time ...

She dropped her head into her hands and didn't see the limousine pass her by. Norah looked up to see the press camped outside Orlando's home and got angry. She got out of the car, slamming the door, her rage alive inside her. "You! Get the fuck away from that door! You do not step one foot on this property without permission. Do you understand?"

Norah rarely got mad, but when she did, the sheer force of her anger made certain that those it was directed at were in no doubt she meant it. Norah pushed past the paparazzi and the news teams and knocked on the front door. Orlando opened it a crack —then his eyes widened in surprise and he threw open the door, grabbed her arm and pulled her inside into a bear hug. Norah held him as he sobbed, his face pressed into her shoulder. Over his shoulder, she saw another younger woman. She could only be Orlando's sister from the resemblance. The woman nodded at her, unsmiling, then disappeared back into the living room.

Orlando released Norah, wiped his face, and tried to smile. "I'm sorry, Norah. I didn't mean to do that. It's so good to see you."

"Orlando ...I can't even begin ..."

"Please," he held up his hand. "I know. Everyone's sorry. Come in and meet some people. See Ferma." He took her hand, starting to draw her into the other room, then stopped, his eyes confused. "Giacomo ..."

A spike of sadness shot through her. Norah braced herself to see her ex-lover, but then Orlando shook his head. "You just missed him. He would have loved to see you, kiddo."

Norah shook her head. 'This isn't about Giacomo and me, Orlando. God, I can't even imagine how you must feel. How's Ferma?"

They walked to the kitchen. "Confused, sad ...she's like the rest of us—in disbelief." Orlando sighed. "When I had to tell her ..."

Norah squeezed his hand. "If there's anything I can do ..." She felt useless, and now she felt like an intruder, but as soon as Ferma saw her, she hugged her tightly.

Orlando introduced Norah to his family and to Carmel's mother, an attractive older woman who looked shattered. Norah couldn't help but hug her. "I'm so sorry."

Norah helped out, cooking for the family, fielding phone calls, and making sure Ferma was fed. Orlando smiled at her gratefully, but Norah kept to herself, not wanting to intrude on the family's grief.

It was getting dark when Norah settled Ferma into bed. The little girl was exhausted and fell asleep, still clutching Norah's hand. In Ferma's other hand was a shirt that Norah recognized as Carmel's. It broke her heart.

She snuck out of the back door, sat on the back steps, and let silent tears fall. What the hell was the matter with this world? Jesus ...

Norah didn't want to attract attention, so she buried her face in her hands and sobbed quietly. After a few minutes, she felt someone sit down beside her and put an arm around her. Somehow, she knew who she would see when she opened her eyes and knew she would have to deal with her heartbreak, but for the moment, she leaned into the warmth of him, breathing in his clean scent. Giacomo pressed his lips against her temple. Neither said anything. There seemed no need for words.

After a while, Norah heard the screen door behind them open. "Take her home, Jack," Orlando's voice was warm and soft. "She's been incredible today. She must be exhausted."

Norah wanted to protest that she wasn't the one who needing taking care of, but suddenly she was overwhelmed with tiredness and sadness. Giacomo nodded and helped her up. Norah hugged Orlando. "I'll come back in the morning if you need me."

Orlando hugged her hard. "You just take care of both of you. We'll be okay. We'll see you soon, right? For the funeral?"

"Of course."

SHE DIDN'T PROTEST when Giacomo led her to his car. There was no way she could drive herself, and, when it became obvious he was driving them back to his place, she felt only relief.

Giacomo took her hand as they walked up the steps and inside and he didn't hesitate to lead her upstairs.

In his bedroom, they faced each other. Giacomo brushed his lips against hers. "Are you tired, Principessa?"

She nodded, but kissed him again, wanting to feel his skin against hers.

'So you want to sleep, mio caro?"

She hesitated only a second before shaking her head. She gazed up at him. His green eyes were ringed with black circles. He looked shattered but still devastatingly handsome. She stroked her fingers down his cheek and he leaned into her touch.

They stripped each other slowly, the heat between them a smoldering thing. This was not the joyful lovemaking of before—this was a desperate need to feel love, closeness, and safety. Feeling his skin against hers was like a drug to Norah and she wanted him to feel some comfort too as they made love slowly.

Afterward, they lay side by side, gazing at each other. Giacomo, in halting tones, told her about the night Carmel was murdered.

"She just lay there, so still, so …it was like everything stopped. I could hear Orlando screaming at her to breathe and yet it sounded like it was coming from a million miles away. Mio Di o…" Giacomo closed his eyes and Norah could see how much he had been affected. "I've never seen so much blood, mio caro,. It was horrific. Did you know she was pregnant?"

"God, no …" Norah's voice broke and she started to cry. Giacomo held her close, his lips against her forehead.

When her sobs quieted, he stroked her damp cheeks. "Bella, this is going to sound monumentally selfish, but all I could think of, once we'd been to the hospital and they'd told us there was nothing they could do, was you. How badly I'd screwed things up by not being completely honest. How short life is."

She nodded, hiccupping her sobs away. Giacomo smiled and kissed her gently. "I'm so sorry, Bella, for not being entirely honest with you from the start. I promise you, my love for you is based solely on us being together and nothing else. I swear it to you."

Norah sighed. "I believe you, Giacomo. At least, I want to. I just need some time is all."

He nodded, though his eyes were sad. "You'll stay tonight?"

She hesitated. She was exhausted and drained and all she wanted was this man's arms around her. Just tonight, she told herself, then we reset. Take our time. She told him that and he looked relieved. She realized then how much he needed her.

"Giacomo," she said, pushing him onto his back and climbing on top of him, "Let's help each other forget for tonight, forget everything except this ..."

She took his hand and guided it between her legs. He stroked her clit and felt how wet she was for him as she trailed her fingers up and down his swelling cock. When he was hard, she slowly impaled herself onto him, sighing with the feeling of being filled by his diamond-hard, thick cock. She rode him slowly at first, but as the tension began to build, he suddenly flipped her onto her back and plunged harder and deeper inside her. Then they were clawing at each other, lips rough against the others, gasping and panting, crying out each other's name.

In the end, neither of them slept, instead fucking until dawn, wanting to savor every moment of each other. Giacomo took her in his bed, on the floor, and in the bathtub until they were both exhausted.

He drove her home through the early morning light, and as she said goodbye, he kissed her tenderly. "Ti amo, mio caro."

She leaned her forehead against his. "I love you too."

· · ·

Norah let herself into Zulika's flat. Ziggy gave a delighted muted woof and came to meet her. She hugged him for a while, then poked her head into Zulika's bedroom. Her friend was still curled up in bed, asleep, so Norah decided not to wake her. She hurriedly scribbled a note for Zulika, telling her they would open the bookstore late to wait for her to wake before going in. As she walked to the bedroom, she checked her phone to see if Orlando had messaged her, but he hadn't.

Then, with Ziggy in tow, Norah fell onto her bed still fully dressed and slept until the afternoon.

CHAPTER NINE

Lucian stared out of the window of the car. He'd asked Tara to meet him, to ask her if she had anything to do with Carmel Price's murder. He had wanted—he had hoped—she would deny it, but she grinned, completely unrepentant, and nodded. "Of course. I told you that situation would be dealt with and it was."

Lucian stared at her in disbelief. "I never said to kill the woman. Jesus, Tara ... she had a kid. The news this morning said she was pregnant and you had her killed for what? Conti already knew about us! Fuck ..."

His voice was growing higher and higher and he saw the sneer on Tara's face. "You wanted the problem to go away and it did."

"Jesus, Tara."

Tara, her icy blonde beauty stone cold, gave a wave of her hand. "That's the only way to deal with the problem. Besides, now Giacomo will be so devastated that he'll need comforting, by someone familiar. Heard he broke up with your girlfriend. Lucky for her."

Lucian went very still. "What do you mean by that?"

Tara stared back coolly. "Exactly what you think."

Lucian raised his hands. "Woah, woah, woah, no. Tara, don't even think about hurting Norah."

Tara shrugged. "Why do you care? You already raped her. Didn't you tell me you told her you'd kill her if she left you? She did leave you. She fucked Giacomo. Why do you care if someone puts a bullet into her?"

Lucian drew in a deep breath. 'Tara ...you want Giacomo back?"

"I do."

"Fine ...then you'll understand that I too wish for something."

Tara cackled loudly. "Are you crazy? That woman will never, ever take you back, Lucian. You raped her. Better she's gone forever, then we can all get on with our lives."

"No!" Lucian was furious now, and before Tara could move, his hands were around her throat, squeezing. She fought back, clawing at his face as she choked.

"Lucian, stop ...I was joking ..."

Lucian seemed to come to his senses. He released her and sat back. "Just know, if any harm comes to Norah ..."

Tara smiled, her fingers touching her throat. "Fine. I must say ...never had you down for a choker, Lucian. Maybe we should explore that side of you next time we meet to fuck."

Lucian gave a disgusted noise. 'Did you understand me when I said no harm comes to Norah?"

"I understood."

"Good. Now, it's best if we don't communicate for a while. I don't want to be tied to Carmel Price's murder."

LUCIAN GOT out of the car and walked back to his own Audi, parked a little way down the street. Tara watched him, the sneer returning to her face. Revolting little punk. She'd only ever fucked him to try and make Giacomo jealous when it seemed like her Italian lover had lost interest in her. Now, though, Lucian had just made things very interesting. If the police ever came looking for her ...she would have no problem in framing Lucian for the murder of his ex-girlfriend. As Tara felt the sore places on her throat again, she smiled. Lucian himself had just signed Norah's death warrant.

"Hello, Bella." For a second Norah, who had been thinking about Giacomo all day, thought she imagined hearing his voice, but when she looked up, there he was, gorgeous in blue jeans and a dark green sweater, smiling as he swaggered to the counter.

She grinned and their eyes met. His smile at seeing her made her want to cry with joy.

Giacomo slid behind the counter and stood next to her, his hand brushing down her hair.

"Hi." His eyes were soft.

"Hi yourself."

They gazed at each other as Zulika came bowling out from the back room and broke the spell.

"Hey, No-No Bear?"

Norah and Giacomo looked at her.

"No? Took me ages to think that up." She looked disappointed.

"You might want to keep working on that." Giacomo shook his head, feigning disapproval.

"MacReddy?"

Norah nodded, mock-disappointment on her face. "Nothing with a 'mac,' please."

Zulika rolled her eyes and grinned at Giacomo. "Hello again. Good to see you."

"You too, shorty."

Zulika looked outraged. "Just because you two are bona-fide giants ..."

Giacomo couldn't help but grin. "That's what the ladies tell me."

Norah snickered. "Modest as always."

Giacomo laughed. Zulika made a gagging noise.

"Jesus, that's not an image I'm comfortable with."

Norah pretended to consider for a moment. "I'm pretty much okay with it." Giacomo made a clicking noise and made finger-pistols at her. Zulika grinned and hoisted herself up onto the counter. Norah and Giacomo looked at each other for a moment, an unspoken agreement taking place. They both looked at Zulika, who grinned back guilelessly.

"Zul?"

"Yes?"

"Go away now. Go grab a coffee down the street."

They waited until a grumbling but smiling Zulika left the bookstore. Norah followed her, locked the door, and flipped the sign. Nervous now, she motioned for Giacomo to follow her into the back room. She was about to speak when he put a finger over her lips.

"Whatever you're about to say ..." He leaned in, hesitated, and then pressed his lips against hers. She sighed and gave in to the kiss, Giacomo moved closer to her and slid a hand onto her stomach, the other onto her back. She held his face in her hands as the kiss deepened. Waves of pleasure shuddered down her body. She felt the warmth of his hands through her dress and slid her own hands into his hair. Giacomo's arms tightened around her, pulling her against his body. Norah couldn't help the small moan of desire that escaped her lips. Giacomo smiled.

"You're beautiful," he whispered against her mouth. His fingers were at the zipper of her dress, gently tugging at it.

"Wait, wait, wait." Norah pulled away, breathless, her voice shaky. Giacomo froze and she felt a pang at the hurt in his eyes.

"I'm sorry ...I can't. Not yet. Giacomo, we need to talk about what happens next." She drew in a long, ragged breath, then laughed softly. "Believe me, there's nothing I'd like more than to ..." She gestured to the floor and they both laughed. Giacomo relaxed and pulled her down to sit on the couch. He smoothed her hair back from her face and she leaned into his touch. Her face was serious.

"If we do this... Giacomo, it has to be for real. No bullshit like last time."

He nodded, his eyes grave. "Anything you need, Norah. Just name it."

She took his face in her hands and kissed him gently. "Time. Just give me time. I need to process this and sort out where my life is going. I need to find my own apartment. You need to deal with Tara ...that side of your life. When we're both free of the past, then yes, Giacomo, I'm yours. I love you. I just have to know you've learned how to face what you need to do and that you can be the man I think you can be. Can you do that for me?"

Giacomo gathered her to him. "Norah, I promise. You don't know how long I've waited for you. With all my heart, I promise. I will never let you down again."

Carmel's funeral was attended by so many people that the small chapel was overrun. Norah felt like an intruder; she had liked Carmel and had grown close to her in a short time, but still, she felt like sitting with Giacomo near the front of the church was depriving someone else of their rightful place.

The whole service was beautiful but desperately sad. Orlando and Ferma clung to each other as the pastor spoke. Giacomo clutched Norah's hand, his other hand was on Orlando's shoulder, supporting him. It made Norah realize how much the two men loved each other. They were family. Norah glanced around. Zulika was at the back of the chapel and she caught Norah's eye. Her tiny shake of the head said everything that was needed to say what she was feeling—what everyone was feeling.

This shouldn't be happening.

Giacomo had told her more about what had happened to Carmel—that she had been shot six times at point-blank range. Merciless. Brutal. Norah couldn't fathom it.

AFTERWARD, everyone gathered at the wake back at Orlando's home, and Norah, Giacomo, and Zulika helped out by organizing everything and making sure the family was taken care of. Driving home, the three of them sat in Giacomo's car silently, each locked in their own thoughts.

Zulika thanked Giacomo for the ride home and looked surprised when Norah followed her out of the car. "Stay with him," she whispered, but Norah shook her head.

"We're taking some space," she told Zulika once they were upstairs in Zulika's apartment, but Zulika sighed.

"Why? Surely today showed that we shouldn't waste time not being with the ones we love." She sounded frustrated and Norah hugged her.

"We're working things out, bubba. Believe me, I want it to work between Giacomo and me. It's just we need to find out more about each other and take a few steps back. Moving in with each other so quickly was a mistake. We don't know each other well enough for it to be …resolved, yet."

Zulika studied her. "Do you trust him?"

Norah gave her a strange smile. "Almost. Now, I'm bushed. I'm going to bed. Night, bubs."

"Goodnight, No-No."

. . .

Zulika lay in bed, unable to sleep. So much had happened lately that she felt exhausted by it all. Not to mention, Zulika had a secret of her own, one she had yet to process. She'd found a lump in her breast a couple of weeks back and had gone to have it checked out. She was due to have a biopsy at the end of the week, but somehow she couldn't bring herself to tell Norah, her best friend, her sister, the one person she would confide in normally. After everything Norah had gone through...no. Better to find out first whether it was anything to worry about. The oncologist had told her she was young to have breast cancer, but there was always the dread of being the exception.

She gave up trying to sleep eventually, and switching her lamp on, grabbed her book and began to read.

Lucian had seen the car pull up and the two women get out. His sister and Norah were dressed entirely in black and he guessed they had been at the lawyer's funeral. That's why he didn't get too angry when he saw who was driving. Did Conti take the women to the funeral as friends? As support?

This time, I'll let it go, he thought to himself. He watched Norah, beautiful in a wrap dress, as she climbed the stairs up to the apartment. *How the hell was I stupid enough to let you go?*

Tara's threats came back to him then, and he couldn't help but picture Norah lying dead, her lovely body riddled with bullets. No. He would not allow Tara to hurt Norah. Norah was his and his alone to decide who she loved and how she lived ...if she lived. He would kill Tara before she could hurt his Norah.

Because the only person who got to decide if Norah died ... was Lucian himself. If she went back to Conti ...if she refused to forgive Lucian ...

Don't make me hurt you, my darling, he thought now, as he watched Norah disappear into the apartment. Don't give me a reason ...please ...

GIACOMO SAT in an endless accounting meeting, not listening to a word anyone said. His mind whirled with everything that was happening outside of the company. Orlando's endless grief; his goddaughter's utter confusion and sorrow. Norah. It had been a week since the funeral and Norah had asked for some time. He'd agreed—of course he had—but he missed her terribly. At least they talked every evening on the phone, sometimes long into the night.

He smiled to himself. Norah had been right. They were learning more about each other now. He discovered she had been labeled a book nerd at school and she wore that badge proudly, that her father's family was from Kerala, India and her mother was a Creole from Louisiana., and that she spoke Hindi, French, and some Russian. He'd sighed at that. "And yet, no Italian. So disappointing."

She'd laughed at his woebegone tone. "I'll try to learn some, I promise."

He'd taught her some that night as they had phone sex. He'd sighed, genuinely this time, and said quite simply, "Bella, voglio essere dentro di te ...I want to be inside you."

He heard her breath quicken. "Norah, would you slide your hand down to your clitoris for me and pretend it's my hand?"

She gave a moan and he knew she had obeyed him. He fisted his cock at the root, sliding his hand up and down, closing his eyes, and pretending it was her hand on him. "Can you feel me, Bella? Can you feel me touching you?"

"Giacomo ..." her voice was a whisper, a moan that sent

blood pulsing through him, the hot rush of it to his cock making him groan.

"Tell me how much you want me, Bella. Tell me as you think about my fingers rubbing you, caressing you, feeling how wet you are for me."

"I want you so badly, Giacomo ..." Norah was panting now.

"My lips are on your nipples, il mio amore, then on your belly, your soft, soft belly, my tongue deep in your navel ...I push my finger inside you...'

A sharp intake of breath, then her moan. "Giacomo, my love, your cock is in my mouth and my tongue is tracing up and down the length of you, tasting you, sucking you ..."

Giacomo felt his cock harden almost painfully at the thought of her warm mouth enveloping it. "I'm going to fuck you harder and longer than you've ever been fucked, Norah ...my cock is pushing inside you now, filling you ...you are mine now. Do you understand?"

"Yes, yes, god ..."

As he felt his orgasm build, he closed his eyes and almost growled down the phone. "I'm going to come inside you, so hard and so long. My seed will fill your belly and mark you as mine ... Norah ...Norah ..."

He heard her cry as she came, her long pants for air, her moaning of his name, and he too peaked, imagining his cum shooting deep inside her or over her beautiful body—her belly, her breasts.

For a few moments, both of them were breathless. Giacomo wanted to be inside her so badly it was killing him, but the mere thought of her responding to just his words was thrilling enough for tonight.

"Anima mio, ti amo. Io e te per sempre, per sempre."

Norah gave a little chuckle. "That's beautiful, my love, what does it mean?'

"My soul, I love you. It is you and me forever, forever." Giacomo knew he shouldn't say 'forever,' but he didn't care. He meant every word.

He heard her breath catch and when she spoke again, her voice broke. "I love you, Giacomo, like I have never loved anything nor anyone before. You are my world. How do you say that in Italian? You are my world?"

Giacomo smiled to himself. "Tu sei il mio mondo."

"Tu sei il mio mondo," she repeated and laughed softly. "Ti amo, Giacomo, Tu sei il mio mondo."

Zulika wished she had told Norah as she sat in the small waiting room at the hospital. In a few minutes, the nurse would take her to see the oncologist, who would push a thin needle into her left breast to draw out a sample—fluid or tissue—to check if it was benign or malignant. She kept telling herself this process over and over so it became familiar and she wouldn't freak out with no one there to calm her down. For the first time in a while, she thought about Lucian. Was there ever a time in their relationship when he would have come with her and supported her?

She almost laughed out loud. Lucian? No freaking way. He hated needles for a start, the loser. Jeez, stop tormenting yourself, she told herself sharply. She toyed with calling Norah and asking her to come sit with her but she figured Norah would be shocked and maybe even angry that Zulika had kept this from her. Zulika could do without the argument right now.

She stepped into the hallway, heading for the water fountain. She bent her head to it, grateful for the cool water.

"Zulika?" She felt a hand on her arm and looked up. Orlando Price was looking at her, his worn, tired eyes friendly. She half-smiled at him, surprised.

"Hey, Orlando ..." She hesitated before giving him a quick hug. "What are you doing here?"

Orlando showed her an envelope. "Picking up some of Carmel's personal belongings. Didn't even think about it before. But ...her wedding ring, you know?"

Zulika's heart ached for him. "Of course."

"Why are you here? Visiting someone?"

For a second, Zulika was discombobulated. She couldn't help glance at the oncology suite door and Orlando followed her gaze. "Zulika?"

"I have a biopsy ...this afternoon." She couldn't help but blurt it out and Orlando looked aghast.

"Oh, god, I'm sorry," he said, then seemed to realize she was really alone. "Is no one with you? Norah?"

Zulika's shoulders slumped. "I didn't tell her. I don't know if it's ...cancer ...or not yet so ..."

"You shouldn't be alone."

"I'll be fine."

"No." He took her arm and led her gently back to the suite. "I'm here. I'm staying."

Zulika wanted to protest that he had enough to deal with, but suddenly the thought of going through this alone made her feel tearful. She smiled up at him. "That would be a comfort. Thank you."

She introduced the oncologist to Orlando and then it was time for the test. Orlando stayed outside the small cubicle, but kept talking to reassure Zulika as she went through the procedure. Afterward, he insisted on taking her to lunch. After they had ordered—the same double stacked burger and sweet potato fries—Zulika studied him.

"You're probably sick of hearing this, but how are you? Really?"

Orlando took a long sip of ice cold soda before he answered.

"Not so good. I guess that's kind of an understatement, but it's been two weeks and I still expect to see Carmel in our bed, or playing with Ferma, or yelling at some junior assistant at the D.A.'s office." He smiled for a second, lost in his thoughts.

"Have the police any idea who would do this?"

He shook his head. "None. They think it was a professional hit because of the bullets used ...god, she never stood a chance. What I keep coming back to is ...she would have told him. She would have told him she was pregnant and he still shot her six times."

Zulika felt sick. She squeezed his arm. "Orlando, I can't even begin to say how sorry I am. If there's anything you need ..."

"Thank you, Zul. God, there's so much in everyday life that I've never had to process before. Where does Ferma go after school when I'm working? Carmel's sister is staying with us, but she has her own family to get back to soon. So I've got to find an afterschool place for her." He smiled at Zulika ruefully. "Sorry. It helps to rant about stuff."

"Rant away," Zulika said as their food arrived and they both fell on the burgers. "God, saturated fat, salt, and red meat."

"Yep, it definitely helps." Orlando half-smiled. "How're things ...at the bookstore?"

Zulika grinned at him properly for the first time. "You mean, have Norah and Giacomo been hooking up?"

Orlando laughed. "Sorry, that wasn't subtle, was it?"

Zulika shrugged good-naturedly. "I don't mind. The official line is ...they're taking things slow and working stuff out. The unofficial line is ...they're as crazy about each other as ever."

"That's good to hear."

"I know."

"You're a good friend to her. I'm sorry about all that business with your brother."

"Step-brother. I keep thinking he's going to pop up and ruin everything for Norah. I feel caught in the middle in that, to my surprise, I feel kind of sorry for Lucian. He lost the best thing that ever happened to him. Saying that, I'll never forgive him for what he did to Norah."

"He should be in jail."

Zulika nodded. "If it were up to me, he would be, but Norah didn't want to go through a trial. Can't blame her for that."

"No, I suppose not."

Zulika shuddered. "How anyone, any woman, could go near that creep is beyond me. The idea of him is so repugnant."

Giacomo nodded. "Not for Tara, though."

Zulika sighed. "No, I suppose not. Want a refill?"

He nodded. Zulika beckoned at the waitress and she filled his coffee mug. Zulika smiled her thanks at her.

"I don't know what her problem is. She too had everything in Giacomo. And now she seems hellbent on tormenting Norah. What a bitch."

"The thing is," Orlando leaned on his elbows, "I don't think Tara really cares for Giacomo. She doesn't love him. She treats him like crap. She just wants to beat Norah, but she can't see that, even without Norah, Giacomo isn't going to take her back. She's in a competition no-one else is playing."

Zulika nodded. "I've met plenty of people like her—the entitlement always boggles my mind. My brother is exactly the same. Norah was just a possession to him."

"Step-brother." Orlando grinned at her and she chuckled.

"Word."

"May I say something?"

"Of course."

"The two of you—you and Norah—and in fact now Giacomo, you move around each other like orbiting moons. Your lives seem to be so intertwined that it appears, from the outside, impossible to break into your little group. Forgive me if

I'm wrong. But it does feel like an exclusive little club. Very hard to penetrate."

Zulika smiled back. "Not at all. You read people well."

"I wonder, did Lucian ever feel like that? Shut out by your and Norah's closeness and your love for each other?"

Zulika was silent. She shrugged eventually. "I can't tell you that, Orlando. Lucian and I were never good friends. But thinking about what you said, yes, maybe there were times he could have felt excluded."

Orlando narrowed his eyes. "What role do you play?"

"What do you mean?"

"There's Giacomo and Norah. Then there's you. Forgive me. We don't know each other that well, but your life must have more going on than constantly refereeing your best friend's sex life and working as a bookseller."

Zulika looked taken aback. "Wow."

Orlando put his hands up and shook his head. "Sorry, that came out way wrong. What I mean is, what about you, Zul? Who looks after you?"

10

CHAPTER TEN

A week later, Norah was working late in the bookstore when she heard someone knocking at the backdoor. A ribbon of fear curled in her stomach. She glanced at the clock. Eleven fifteen at night.

"Who is it?"

"It's me, mio caro."

Her body relaxed immediately and she opened the door to see Giacomo holding a pizza box and grinning at her. "I know this is breaking the rules, but to hell with it. I was missing you."

Norah laughed. "Get in here, Conti. You're forgiven, mostly because you brought food." She kissed him and took the box from him. "For future reference, that will always work, by the way." She winked at him as he laughed.

"Thanks for the tip. How are you, Bella?" He opened his arms and she went into them without hesitation.

"Better now." She nuzzled her nose against his before pressing her lips to his. The kiss went on longer than either of them expected and by the time they broke apart, both were so turned on that it seemed only natural to start stripping each other.

"I really hope you locked that door." Giacomo grinned and Norah laughed. Her hands were running over his finely-planed chest, her fingertips tracing the dark circles of his nipples.

"Why, sir, we're only making out."

Giacomo raised an eyebrow and his smile hitched up at one side. "Is that so? In that case, Ms. Reddy, I guess I'll just have to tell you how beautiful you are." His hand slipped into her panties and started to caress her. Norah gave a small moan, closing her eyes. He kissed each eyelid.

"...how much I love you ..." He nuzzled her neck and his fingers increased their pressure on her clit. "This is my new definition of making out, Norah Reddy."

Norah laughed, her breath coming in little gasps now. Gently moving her down to the floor, Giacomo bent his head and whispered into her ear.

"Norah, Norah, Norah ..."

Giacomo smiled as she came, trembling and sighing his name. He bent his head and kissed her, feeling her press herself against him.

She caught her breath and smiled at him, her face flushed, and glowing. "Wow. Giacomo Conti, I think I like your new definition of making out." She pushed him onto his back and stroked his face. "I think maybe it's my turn to add a new definition."

"You do, mio caro?"

"Oh, yeah." Grinning, she moved down his body. Sliding her fingers under the waistband of his underwear, she slowly peeled them back, smiling as his enormous, rock-hard cock sprang up. She took him into her mouth, tasting the salty pre-cum and sensing him tensing as she teased the sensitive tip. "Tell me what you like, Giacomo."

He groaned as she began to suck at him, drawing her mouth up and down his shaft. "Mio Dio, Bella, the warmth of your mouth on me ...it is as sweet as any touch. I only compare it to the feeling of my cock deep inside your delicious cunt, deeper and deeper into you ...Norah ..."

She would not release him as he neared his peak and he came hard, shooting his seed into her throat. She swallowed him down and smiled up at him. "I love you, Giacomo."

Still panting, he pulled her up so he could kiss her mouth, then pushed her onto her back, pushing her legs apart and burying his face in her sex. Gently but relentlessly, his tongue and his fingers brought her to orgasm, and then his cock was plunging deep inside her as she was still coming and she screamed with pleasure as he fucked her. He pushed her legs to her chest, desperate to get as deep as he could inside her. Norah's fingernails dug deep into his back; their lips sought the other's almost desperately.

They made love with fire, a ferocity that surprised both of them. Their gazes were fixed, completely locked onto each other, focused and intense.

They fucked against the wall of the bookshop, on the couch, and upstairs in the little shower room. Finally, utterly spent, they lay together on the couch, not needing words. As dawn began to break over the city, they fell asleep in each other's arms.

"Ahem."

Giacomo and Norah woke with a start. Zulika was grinning down at them. Giacomo jumped up, grabbing the couch cushions and shielding himself. Norah started laughing at him and Zulika hid her eyes.

"I'm officially horrified at seeing you both naked." She grinned at Norah, who was giggling helplessly at Giacomo not being able to find his pants. Zulika went out into the bookstore.

"There's underwear all over this place," she yelled. Norah

wandered in, followed by a swaggering Giacomo. "You did it in here? Dudes, there're perfectly good beds in both your houses. What if Health and Human Services found out?"

Norah shrugged and Giacomo grinned.

"Live with it, Zul. Sometimes you gotta do what you gotta do when you gotta do it."

"Huh?" Zulika shook her head.

Norah gave a filthy snigger, pulling on her jeans and handing Giacomo back his shirt.

"Sorry, Zul, sometimes these things take you over."

Zulika looked into the sky. "Ah, youth."

"Grandma. Look, I don't suppose you'd hold down the fort while we go ...um ...tidy ourselves?"

Zulika nodded. "Sure thing ...but I do have an appointment this afternoon."

Norah kissed her cheek. "Promise I'll be back way before then." She grinned at Giacomo and held out her hand. "Coming home with me?"

Zulika watched them walk out together, chatting and laughing. It made her heart warm to see them so happy. Maybe everything will be okay. She swallowed hard. The oncologist had called her that morning, wanting her to come see him. "Today, please, Miss Hargity."

So soon there was never good news. Zulika closed her eyes. Cancer? Really? At her age? She suddenly felt tearful, her whole body trembling. I wish you were still here, Mom, she thought. I need you right now.

She went out back and retrieved her phone, flipping through the contacts. She hesitated when she saw his number. Orlando had enough problems without her leaning on him for this ...

Except ...he had called her every night, asking how she was. They'd been leaning on each other. Her finger hovered over the call button for just a second longer, then she dialed.

The second she heard his voice, his warm, deep, kind voice, it brought the tears.

"What is it, sweetheart?" He said, and in a broken voice, she told him. There was a brief silence on the other end of the phone. Then he cleared his throat.

"What time is your appointment?"

She told him. "Okay," he said, determinedly. "I'll come pick you up and we'll go together. You should not be alone at a time like this."

"I can't begin to thank you, Lando," she said. "I feel awful having to ask."

"Don't be silly. It's no trouble. I want to be there for you, Zul."

"You are a great friend. Thank you."

"I'll see you at two o'clock."

After they had said goodbye, Zulika sat for a while on the couch and took some deep breaths. Finally, composed, comforted by the thought of Orlando being with her, she went to work and opened the bookstore.

"LET me up off of this bed," Norah said, chuckling as Giacomo, naked once more, lay on top of her. "We can't stay in bed screwing all day. Your business empire will crumble and my business partner needs help in the store."

Giacomo, unrepentant, didn't move. "No. You are my prisoner now, Reddy."

She rolled her eyes, giggling. "Yes, I can feel your ...um ...nightstick. I'm beginning to think it's permanently at full mast."

Grinning, he thrust his cock back into her and she gasped. "God, you are insatiable."

"When it comes to you, yes ..."

Norah gave in as he began to thrust harder. She would never

get tired of making love with this man; at least, her mind wouldn't. Her body was getting extra work outs that it wasn't expecting these days.

Afterward, they showered together, and as they were dressing, she could see Giacomo's eyes on her body, lust-filled and intense. It made her feel sexy and wanted. She asked him to pull the zipper up on the back of her summer dress and sighed happily as she felt his lips against her spine. When he'd fastened her dress, he slid his arm around her waist, splaying his hands over her belly and pulling her back into him.

'Il mio amore,' he murmured in her ear, 'Sei tutto per me. Sei la mia vita." My love, you are everything to me. You are my life.

Norah's eyes filled with tears and she turned in his arms. "Never let me go," she said, her eyes soft with love.

Giacomo nodded, his face lit up by his smile. "I promise, Bella. Never."

ZULIKA FELT her whole body shut down with the shock. She barely felt Orlando's hand holding hers. Cancer. Stage III.

This cannot be happening.

Dr. Miller, the oncologist, was looking at her with sympathy. "It is very rare for someone your age, but it does happen."

Zulika blinked. "Did I do something wrong?"

She felt Orlando's hand tighten around hers. "Of course not, Zulika. It's just rotten bad luck."

"Mr. Price is correct. You cannot have seen this coming. Now, look, I've given you the bad news. The worst of it. So now let's look at the positives ...and I promise you, they outweigh the bad. First, there's your youth and your excellent health and fitness. We are at what we call Stage IIIa; your tumor isn't large, but it has spread to a few lymph nodes. The good news is, we can operate and there are several treatments we can try going forward. We found it before it spread too far or became inoperable."

Zulika nodded along, glancing at Orlando for reassurance. Suddenly she felt a pang of guilt. This man had just lost his wife in the most horrific way ...and he was here, comforting her. She turned back to the doctor.

"When can we start? I'm assuming there's also things I can do myself to help ...diet, exercise?"

"Sure," the doctor nodded, smiling at her. "That's a good attitude, Zulika. Let's go through some options now and start on a plan."

ONCE AGAIN, Orlando insisted on taking her to supper afterward. "If you don't mind, though, I do have to pick Ferma up from the sitter first."

"Of course not ...look, I don't want to intrude."

"You won't be at all. Both Ferma and I would welcome the company."

She studied him as he drove back towards his neighborhood. "How are you and Ferma coping? Really?"

He sighed. "Some days are worse than others. Ferma keeps asking questions about how mommy died."

"What did you tell her?"

"At first, I didn't know how ...I was all for the whole mommy got sick very quickly thing, but then my sister, Claudette—I think you met her at the funeral—told me that kids at Ferma's school had heard the truth. So I had to tell her that someone murdered Mommy. She wants to know why. That's the one thing I couldn't answer."

He sounded so heartbroken that it made Zulika's breath freeze in her lungs.

After a long silence, she tried to smile at him. 'Listen, seeing as we're almost at your house anyways, how about I cook for all three of us? Is that too presumptuous?"

Orlando smiled at her. "Not at all. We'd welcome your company. It's just, I don't know what we have at home."

Zulika waved her hand. "Don't worry about that. I have a gift for inventing recipes with whatever's available. Ask Norah. Many a night, especially in college, we've had Le Coq au Vin Ramen—that one was ramen noodles, chicken soup, and beer. Surprisingly good."

Orlando was laughing now. "Please tell me you've never used Ziggy's food to make a stew?"

"It's come close a couple of times," she laughed, "Norah is very suspicious these days. She swore blind that a Bourguignon I made this one time was with 'Extra Beefy Chunks' out of a Nature's Recipe can. I wouldn't have minded, but I slaved over that stew."

Orlando was laughing loudly. "I'm so glad I don't have pets right now."

She grinned at him. "You should be."

Orlando looked around at her, and for once, he looked happy. "Anyway, you have a deal. Besides, we have pizza delivery on stand-by just in case."

"Oh ye of little faith."

NORAH, after Zulika had left for the afternoon, had immersed herself in her work, only distracted by the memories of Giacomo's hands on her body. She was still thinking about that, shoving new deliveries out on the shelves, when she heard the tinkle of the shop's door bell.

She turned to greet her customer and her heart failed.

"What are you doing here?"

Lucian held his hands up, not approaching her. "Just to talk,

Norah. That's all, I swear. I'll stay over here."

Norah, not trusting him, darted behind the counter and picked up her scissors. Her phone was in the back, shoved deep into her purse, and she cursed herself for not keeping it with her. She eyed Lucian warily. "We had an agreement, Lucian. You're breaking it. If I call the police now, you'll be back in jail before you blink."

He nodded. "I know and I realize I'm taking a risk here. I just wanted to see you. Baby, I miss you."

"Well, I don't miss you," she shot back. "Please leave."

"Sweetheart, I'm just here to apologize. For everything. For what I did to you. For fucking Tara Hubert. I should have realized what I had when I had it."

Norah's expression hardened. "But you didn't. You don't get a do-over, Lucian. I've moved on."

His smile was patronizing. "I heard. With Tara's ex, I see."

Norah said nothing. Her hand was resting on the scissors, ready to use them as a weapon. Lucian glanced at them, putting his head on the side and smiling at her. "You won't need those, darling. I swear, I just came to talk."

"I'm not interested.'" Norah moved around the counter and went to the door, opening it. "Get out. Now."

Lucian gave a long-suffering sigh. "Well, I tried. Could you at least pass on my regards to my sister? She's the only family I have left, after all."

Norah wasn't moved. "Entirely your doing, Lucian. Please leave."

He walked toward her and she tensed, but he simply stepped out of the door. He turned, however, stopped her from closing it, and said. "I loved you. I still love you. I'm not done."

Norah looked at him bleakly. "I don't think you know what love is, Lucian. It isn't rape. It isn't threats and violence. My advice to you is be done. Because I'm never, ever coming back to you. I am so done."

He moved quickly, pushing her up against the wall, his lips rough on hers. Norah cried out as his fingers pressed hard into her belly, his other hand groping her breast. She struggled with him and, finally, he let her go.

"Get the fuck out now, or I swear to god, I will throw your ass in jail." She was panting, her rage easily quelling any fear.

Lucian smirked. "Just giving you a taste of a real man."

Norah started to laugh. "Oh, you poor deluded piece of shit. You are about as far from a real man as exists." She brought her knee up and smashed into his groin. As he groaned, she pushed him out of the door and double locked it. "I'm calling the police right now, so you'd better run. Oh, and for the record, go fuck yourself."

Norah was as angry and as riled up as she'd ever been as she yelled at him. She went to the backdoor, checking that it was locked, and grabbed her phone, going back out front to check that Lucian was gone. She saw him limping to his Audi and when he turned to look back as he got into his car, she gave him the finger and waved the phone at him.

God, that had felt so good. She realized all the anger and hurt she had been harboring since Lucian raped her had been released and for the first time she could breathe freely.

She laughed softly as she called Giacomo and asked him to come pick her up. "I'm sorry I wasted so much time, baby. I love you. If you'll still have me, I'd love to move in with you."

LUCIAN DROVE to Land's End Park and then stopped the car. He'd nearly lost it—nearly ripped the knife he had hidden from his pocket and slammed it into her, his anger at the rejection overwhelming. It took every last piece of his control not to kill her. Bitch. Fucking whore bitch. He looked back along the road. Should he go back now? Finish this? No. He got out of the car and walked into the park, needing to walk or jog his anger off. He sucked in huge breaths, waiting for his control to return. No. Too many people had seen him drive to the bookstore; probably the neighbors had heard Norah yelling at him. If she had called the police, they would come looking for him immediately, if they weren't already. Fucking bitch ... If she were murdered tonight, it would all be over. All his careful planning. Lucian closed his eyes. His reason was returning. A simple slaughter wasn't enough. Too easy. Death could wait. There were more interesting things to do to her first. Punishment. Suffering. Humiliation. Violation. Pain. And he knew exactly who would help him do it all.

Tara. His mind made up, Lucian smiled. Norah—and everyone she loved—would soon wish they had never been born.

FOUR MONTHS LATER ...

GIACOMO TRAILED his lips down Norah's spine as they lay in his bed, the early morning sun shining down on her café-au-lait skin. He had honestly never thought he was capable of being this wiped out by love, but this beautiful, sweet, smart, funny girl had invaded his every waking thought. These last few months had been deliriously happy. He had persuaded her to return to working with him, and she had risen to the challenge, growing in confidence and impressing his board. The word had gotten out too and Norah had found herself on the end of some very interesting offers.

Giacomo pressed his lips to the back of her neck as she slept.

She had resisted the offers at first, wanting, he suspected, to prove to him that she was loyal, but he had encouraged her to take the meetings at least. They would both work long hours, then come home to each other, cook together, then talk before going to bed and making love late into the night. He sometimes wondered when they had time to sleep. Their weekends were sacrosanct, spent either with each other at home, lazing around and staying in bed late, or with Orlando, Ferma, and more often than not now, Zulika, who had become great friends with Orlando and his daughter.

Giacomo was grateful to Zulika for distracting Lando and Ferma from their dreadful grief and the frustration of not knowing who killed Carmel and why. The police simply had no leads and Giacomo had thrown his influence and money behind a private investigation, but so far had come up empty.

"Whatever you need to do to find the answers, do it." he'd told the head of his team, fixing him with a look. The head of security, who had known Giacomo since he was a kid, nodded.

"Gotcha, boss. Anything goes."

He was so lost in his thoughts, he hadn't noticed that Norah had awoken and was watching him, a small smile playing around her lips. "Hello, baby."

He smiled down at her. "Buongiorno, il mio amore."

She turned onto her back and stretched like a cat, and Giacomo admired her curves with relish. She grinned at him as he ran a hand down her belly. "What were you thinking about?"

"Lando ...and how much Zulika has helped him and Ferma."

Norah smiled. "I know, right? Still, I wish I could wave a magic wand and bring Carmel back. Zul told me that Ferma is being bullied at school for not having a mommy."

Giacomo made a disgusted noise. "Is there anyone crueler than a kid?"

Norah laughed slightly. "Cruel people are cruel, no matter

their age. If their parents taught them proper values ...look at me, ranting like I know what the hell I'm talking about."

"You don't talk much about your family," he said, pressing his lips against her shoulder. Norah shrugged, not fazed by his question. "We weren't particularly close growing up. My mom brought me here when she divorced my father and we never saw him again. Mom died when I was seventeen. Zulika was the nearest thing to family. Now, of course, I have you, Lando, and Ferma, and my friends. Our friends."

"Very true, Principessa." He gazed down at her. "Did you ever consider Hargity as family?"

"Ha. No, not even when I thought I was in love with him. Ugh, the mere thought of him makes me retch. Still, he seems to have taken the hint after the last time he tried to weasel his way in."

"What?"

"Oh." Norah stopped and went red. "Yeah, I might have forgotten to mention that. He came to the store one evening, trying to pretend he was a reformed character and that he still loved me. That he wanted me back."

"Did he hurt you?"

"No ...he tried to ..."

Before she could finish, Giacomo growled and leaped out of the bed.

Alarmed, Norah sat up. "What are you doing?"

"I'm gonna find him and then I'm going to fucking kill, the figlio di puttana." He was halfway out of the door, wild with rage. Norah grabbed him and dragged him back into the room.

"Norah, no. Let me go."

"Stop. Stop."

She got his face in her hands and made him look at her. His eyes were mad.

"Stop. Let me finish. He tried to kiss me, is all. I stopped him."

Giacomo closed his eyes and sucked in a huge breath. After a few breaths, he looked at her, hurt written across his face. "He could have killed you."

"But he didn't."

"But you decided not to tell me?"

"Yes."

He leaned his forehead against hers. "Don't do that again. Why didn't you tell me?"

"I didn't want you going off at him and getting into trouble. I'm not losing you because of him. Because of anything. I imagined you ending up in San Quentin for the rest of your life." She kissed him. "Anyway, I had better things to do than worry about that skid-mark."

Giacomo half-smiled at that. "Still, it was really stupid of you not to tell me."

"I know. It was dumb."

"Really dumb." He sighed and sat on the bed studying her. She stroked his hair near his temple, feeling his body relaxing as she caressed him. His green eyes were still troubled as he gazed at her.

"How did you get rid of him?

Norah grinned at him. "I smashed my knee into his junk."

Giacomo started to laugh. "You did?"

"Hard, too. He folded like a wet watermelon. Really fucking satisfying it was, too."

Giacomo, still chuckling, kissed her. "Bad-ass mother."

"Yes, I am." She wrapped her arms around his neck. "Do you know what I felt that day?"

"Tell me."

"I wasn't scared anymore. Not of him, nor of anything. I felt free. Because you love me. Because I knew you had my back."

He smiled and sat on the floor, pulling her down on top of him. "Always." He grinned. "And now I have your back, your front, and your sides."

"Funny boy." She kissed him, sliding her hand down to cup his thickening cock. She grinned wickedly. "Now, be a good boy and put that inside me."

Giacomo laughed and pushed her onto her back, hitching her legs around his hips. "You're getting very bossy, Ms. Reddy ... maybe we should invest in some fun equipment to play with."

"Ooo, I like that idea," she said, arching her back as he kissed her belly, rimming her navel with his tongue. "Then I could really be your boss in the bedroom."

"I may permit it," he said and laughed at her mock-outrage, "Oh, you want to argue with that, mio caro? Then you'd better take this ..." He thrust his cock deep into her, and she gasped and laughed as he proceeded to fuck her hard, grinning the whole time.

CHAPTER ELEVEN

Zulika felt the nausea come again and headed to the bathroom to throw up for the third time that morning. Orlando was waiting outside the door with some water and a cold press for her head.

He had offered her the spare room in his house while she was going through chemo, and although she had resisted at first, when the side effects had kicked in properly, she was glad of the support. Often she had thought how strange it was that the three of them existed in this weird life together, but more and more, it seemed natural. She and Ferma got along so well that she knew Ferma thought of her as a big sister, and Zulika had enjoyed caring for the girl when Orlando couldn't get home in time for her. Ferma's school was only two blocks from the bookstore, so Zulika would go and fetch her and bring her back to sit with Ziggy, a glass of cold milk, cookies, and any book Ferma wanted to read. Thanks to Ferma, they had increased their children's section and now more kids would come in to read after school. Zulika loved being around them all; they gave her hope.

Because the cancer was worse than they had thought. It had progressed to Stage IIIb, which meant more surgery, and more chemo. Zulika couldn't quite believe that she was sick—most days she felt fine, which is how she managed to keep it from Norah. Thankfully, in Zulika's mind, Norah was so happy and so caught up with Giacomo that Zulika only had to hide it from her when they were together, which was getting rarer and rarer with the amount of work they both had. Orlando had tried to persuade her to tell Norah, citing the evenings they spent with their friends where Lando and Zulika had to maintain the secret. Ferma, who adored both Giacomo and Norah, was also ignorant of the cancer. Orlando had to field some inquiries from curious relatives about why he had moved another woman into his home. They had settled on telling them that Zulika was both a tutor and caregiver for Ferma. But everything seemed like an enormous obstacle to be overcome and Zulika felt worn down by it all.

The one bright spot was Orlando. He'd distracted her by asking her to tell him stories about herself, Norah, and their happy times together. He hung out at the bookstore with her and Ferma, making them laugh and charming the customers. He didn't mention Lucian once or what had happened, never once looked at her with anything other than friendship. She was glad. Both of them were still so damaged—Orlando still so lost in grief for his dead wife—that anything else would have been both wildly inappropriate and awkward. He was, however, quickly becoming her confidante. They would talk about everything, however painful, for hours in the evenings after Ferma was in bed. He had even cried in front of her, something he told her he never did in front of other people, not even Giacomo.

Today Orlando would accompany her to the oncologist's office for the results of the latest tests. After the scans, the x-rays, and the chemo, she desperately needed to hear good news and, not only that, it was a big day. If the news was good, she was going to tell Norah tonight at dinner. If not, normal service would resume.

Orlando looked over at her as he drove them to the appointment. He smiled. "I just have a feeling we're going to hear good news."

She squeezed his hand gratefully. "I hope so."

Norah looked up as the door to the shop opened. Giacomo came in, grinning, and she laughed. "Dude, seriously, your business is going to go kaput unless you spend more time there."

Giacomo smiled, shrugging good-naturedly. "This time I have an excuse. We have been summoned. I am to drive us both to Orlando's house for supper. Queen Ferma requests our presence."

Norah's eyes bugged out of her head when she saw Zulika emerging from Orlando's house to greet them, Orlando at her side, looking for all the world like a happy couple.

"Holy moly." Norah grinned and Giacomo rolled his eyes.

"Bet it isn't what you think."

She made a sour face at him. "Well, aren't you just Mr. Glass Half Empty?" Giacomo laughed and pulled up alongside the curb. Norah was antsy now to get the gossip. Getting out of the car, Giacomo wrapped his arms around her, sniggering to himself as he maintained the hug too long and she started to giggle.

"Gerroff me, you big Italian lug," she complained as he laughed out aloud. She hugged Zulika, noticing for the first time how thin she had gotten. "How are you, gorgeous?"

Orlando's grin was earsplitting. "Well, that's what we have to tell you. Come inside."

Norah was almost dying of curiosity now. Were Orlando and Zulika together? Her oldest friend looked remarkably comfortable in Orlando's home. But Norah couldn't believe that Orlando would want to be in a relationship so soon and Zulika, she knew, would balk at starting up with someone in his position.

"What's going on?" She looked between Zulika and Orlando.

Zulika took her friend's hands. "Okay ...well, look. I have something to tell you, No-No, and I don't want you to be angry at me. Please just hear me out."

Norah's heart began to thump unpleasantly against her ribs. "God, Zul ...what?"

Zulika took a deep breath in. "Pull off the Band-Aid. Okay, Norah, Giacomo, I have cancer."

Both them of them stared at her dumbly. "What? No, no, no." Norah couldn't breathe. "No, it can't be. You're too young. It's not right."

Zulika tried to smile. "Stage III breast cancer. Now, I've had surgery to remove the tumor, and chemo, and ..."

"Wait, how long have you known?"

Zulika bit her lip. "About five months."

"Five months!" Norah felt her heart plummet. "God, and you've been through this on your own? You didn't tell me?"

"You were going through some stuff of your own, remember?"

Norah's eyes widened. "Zul! What the hell? Do you think I wouldn't have dropped everything for you?"

Zulika half-smiled. "That's why I didn't tell you. You have every right to be angry."

"This isn't about me! You needed ..."

"Why do you think I'm telling you with Lando here? He's been my rock."

Orlando spoke then, his voice wracked with sorrow. "And

Zul's been mine. How Ferma and I would have gotten through these last months …yes, the circumstances were the worst, but I think—I hope—both Zulika and I have gained strength from helping each other."

Zulika smiled at him gratefully. "I certainly have. Norah, I'm sorry. Yes, in times past, we would have been there for each other. This time, we both needed other people. I think it's healthy. Forgive me, darling, but I stand by my decision."

Norah was silent for a long time. Giacomo put his hand on the back of her neck, rubbing it reassuringly. Finally, she nodded. "So, now that we all know, what can we do?"

"Well, first thing is …we don't make it the sole topic of conversation whenever we meet." Zulika grinned at her friends. "We all have stuff we need to work through. So it's fine to mention it, but not to dwell. Agreed?"

The other murmured their assent. "Good. Now, to let you know the good news. I went to the oncologist today. The treatment is working. The cancer went to some lymph nodes, but it hasn't spread and the main tumor hasn't reappeared."

Norah let out a long breath. "Thank god."

"So you see? We can overcome anything." She looked at Orlando then. "Your turn."

Giacomo sat up straight as Orlando began to speak. "The police are closing the investigation."

"No! No way," Norah exclaimed as Giacomo, looking angry, shook his head.

"I don't believe it."

"They say they've exhausted every lead and every suspect. They can't spend any more money on it."

"Fuck them!" Giacomo was up now, pacing. "Lando, I promise you, I will never stop trying to find Carmel's killer."

Orlando looked at him gratefully. "I would tell you I can't let you spend your money, but I know it won't make a difference."

"It won't."

"Thank you, my friend."

Zulika sighed. "Look, shall we eat? Ferma will be home from school soon and she'll be starving."

Orlando stood. "We're barbecuing," he said, moving to the French windows. "I've already set it up."

"I'll give you a hand." Giacomo followed his friend outside, leaving the two women alone. Norah got up and went to her friend and they hugged for a long time.

"Love you, Zully."

"Love you too, Batfink."

Norah giggled. "Batfink?"

"Orlando has them all on—guess what—video tape. And he still has a video machine!"

Both of them broke into giggles, and when Orlando came to tell them the barbecue grill was ready for the chicken, both Zulika and Norah had to bite their lips. "Chicken?" Norah pretended to be serious. "Have you thought of branching out on the meat you grill? Say ...bat?"

Orlando rolled his eyes. "I knew that wouldn't stay secret for long. Yeah, so I liked Batfink. What can I tell you?"

Giacomo stuck his head in the door. "What the hell are you talking about?"

Norah stood and went to her lover. "A kid's show us poor Americans had to suffer through."

Orlando scoffed as he herded them all outside. "Philistines."

THE EVENING PASSED PLEASANTLY, even happily. Ferma came home, delighted to see her godfather and Norah. By the end of the evening, when Giacomo and Norah were saying goodbye, it felt like a family had been together again.

As Zulika hugged her friend, she suddenly remembered

something. "Hey, before I forget, we need to talk about the bookstore. I think we're at the point where we need to take someone else on."

Norah nodded. "I think you're right. I'm sorry I've been leaving it all to you, Zul. Look, I'll come in tomorrow and we'll put together an ad."

Zulika grinned. "Don't apologize. I'm psyched that your business has taken off. Soon you'll be too fancy to visit the likes of us."

Norah cocked her little finger and pretended to sip some tea. "What do you mean 'soon?'"

"Doofus."

Norah chuckled. "Listen ...anything you need, Zul, ask. I'm always here."

"I know that. Love you, girl."

"Love you too, girl."

ZULIKA HELPED Orlando tidy up the backyard. "Lando ...I think I need to try and get back to some sort of independent living, you know? Now that things are looking up? Not that I'm not grateful for everything, and believe me, I'll still be here every day for you and Ferma."

Orlando nodded. "Well, we knew this was temporary, yes? But, still, we'll miss you."

"And I you. I'm not saying I'll want to move out entirely at the start ...maybe a couple of days a week for a while to get on my feet? The weekends, maybe, when you're at home for Ferma?"

Orlando sighed, but smiled. "That sounds like a good idea."

Zulika hesitated. "Lando ...nothing will change between me and you and Ferma. You are my family now. I just need to try and regain some of my old life."

Orlando put down the plates he was holding and came to her. He pulled her into a hug. "You don't need to justify yourself to me, Zul. I think you should; it'll bring you some confidence."

They cleared away the mess together in a companionable silence. Before she said goodnight, she paused at the bottom of the stairs. "It doesn't have to be just yet, Lando."

Orlando's smile was warm. "It can be whenever you feel ready. As far as I'm concerned ...this is your home too."

Much, much later, Zulika would realize that was the moment when she fell in love with him.

THE GIRL, not older than eighteen, had rainbow-colored hair, tattoos, and a broad grin. "Like I said, I ain't had too much experience since leaving school, but I love books more than anything. Give me Harper Lee or Jack Kerouac over the telly anytime."

Her broad Cockney accent sounded strange in this most American of surroundings, but Norah and Zulika shared a glance and a smile. The girl—"Fred. That's what I prefer. Call me Freda and I won't answer. Stupid bloody name."—had walked in off the street. They'd actually witnessed her doing a body swerve when she saw the 'hiring' notice in the window. She was a regular customer, had chatted with both Norah and Zulika on occasion, and now the two women knew they had found their new colleague.

"When can you start, Fred?" Zulika said warmly and watched as the girl's eyes widened.

"Really?"

Norah grinned. "Really. You had us at 'wotcha,' whatever that means."

Fred laughed. "It's London for 'Hiya.' God, thank you so much. I'm so fucking excited. Whoops, sorry."

Zulika rolled her eyes. "It's fine. Just not in front of the customers. So, seriously, when can you start?"

"Right now, if you like."

They laughed. "How about in the morning?" Norah said and Zulika nodded. Fred hesitated then hugged them both.

"Seriously, dudes, thank you. I have all the visa stuff I need. Shall I bring it in?"

Zulika nodded. "Do, and we'll do all the paperwork we need to. So, welcome to Anthology."

AFTER FRED, who was obviously excited as hell, had left, Norah looked at her friend. "How are you feeling?"

Zulika hid a smile. It was the third time that morning that Norah had asked. "I'm good. Really good, I promise. I've been spending some time back at my apartment, getting used to being independent again. I miss Lando and Ferma, but I think it's something I need to do."

Norah smiled. "I bet they miss your cooking."

Zulika laughed. "Lando's actually a much better cook than me. All I do, really, is remember all the Indian food you taught me how to make and try to recreate it. Sometimes it works better than others. Ask Lando about the fish curry …yeah, that was an adventure."

Norah laughed. "I shudder to think. How's he doing?"

"Frustrated that the police have given up on finding Carmel's killer."

"Giacomo's got his men on it."

"They find anything?"

Norah grimaced, shook her head. "Unfortunately, no. Not yet."

There was a long silence. "Have you heard from Lucian again? Lando told me that he'd been bothering you."

Norah sighed. "Not since I mangled his junk with my knee, thank god. Maybe he's finally taken the hint."

"Let's hope."

Norah left Zulika alone and went up to her office to sort through some emails. Her schedule was filled through to the end of the year, and for a moment, she felt overwhelmed. *This is what you have worked for, Reddy*, she told herself and drew in a long breath. She pulled up the details of the three contracts she was working on: one for a designer clothing store in the city, another for a cosmetics company, and the last and biggest, the one which would make her name, a campaign for one of San Francisco's most exclusive boutique hotels. On that one, she would be working with an advertisement agency who had connections worldwide. If she could nail it, her network would grow exponentially.

She set about outlining her ideas, doing rough sketches of what she envisioned, and before long, it was late afternoon and Zulika had come to say goodbye.

"Have to pick the munchkin up from school," Zulika told her as she pulled on her jacket. It was late spring, but a cold front had rolled in from the ocean. She kissed the top of Norah's head. "Don't work too late; that gorgeous man will be waiting for you."

Norah chuckled. "Yeah, like old workaholic Giacomo will leave work this early. Have a good night, Zul, and kiss Ferma and Lando for me."

She was surprised to see two pink spots of blush appear on Zulika's cheeks when she mentioned Lando, but, clearly embarrassed, Zulika merely smiled and waved goodbye.

Norah put her pencil down and went to make some fresh coffee. She wondered about Zulika and Lando. Going through all that trauma had certainly brought them closer, and now, based on Zulika's reaction just now, Norah wondered just how close it had brought them. She chewed her lip as she brought the steaming cup of coffee back to her desk. She hoped neither would get hurt if something was going on; they were both so vulnerable at the moment.

It's none of your concern. Don't interfere. She could almost hear Giacomo's voice and smiled to herself.

Her email pinged and she opened it up to see an email from the contact at the advertising agency. As she read it, her heart sank.

DEAR MS. REDDY,

FURTHER TO OUR conversations regarding the Temple Bliss Hotel project, I am writing to inform you that, unfortunately, the company has asked us to remove you from the project.

We are not entirely sure why this is and we apologize for any inconvenience caused. You will, of course, be fully compensated for your time and the work already undertaken.

Please note that as an agency, we cannot enter into any discussion of why this has occurred, and as we are still employed by The Temple Bliss organization, I would ask you please to be discreet and remember the non-disclosure agreement that we all signed.

Please accept, again, my apologies and my wishes for your future success.

YOURS,

. . .

Peter O'Flynn
C.E.O.
Harlequin Advertising

NORAH STARED BLANKLY at the screen. "I've just been fired." She said it aloud to make sure it sunk in. She'd never been fired from anything in her life. What the hell had happened? Why had they asked for her specifically to be taken off the project? She couldn't help but feel the sting. Was it because she was inexperienced? No, it couldn't be—the status that working with Giacomo had brought her had been immeasurable. Was it that her romantic relationship with Giacomo was starting to be noticed and commented on? No, again, Giacomo's good name and social standing would never hold her back. She hated even thinking like that. Giacomo could work in a chop shop and she'd love him the same.

She felt her chest get heavy with the disappointment. She drove home a little while later, still chewing it over.

Giacomo's smile faded when she walked into their kitchen to find him already cooking. "What is it, Bella?"

She told him and he put down the knife he was using to chop vegetables, wiped his hands, and took her in his arms.

"I'm sorry, mio caro."

She sighed, leaning into him and feeling the solid warmth of his big body. "I know these things happen. It's just a blow, is all."

Giacomo pressed his lips to her temple. "I know."

They embraced for a few minutes, then Norah pulled away, forcing a smile onto her face. "That smells delicious …what have we got tonight?"

"Ginger-glazed Mahi-Mahi, fresh green beans, and asparagus."

Norah was impressed. "Fancy. Sounds delicious." She

hoisted herself onto the counter and watched him cook. She loved the way his dark curls were always in disarray and how his light-green eyes were so intense on whatever he was concentrating on. She grinned to herself and he noticed.

"What?"

She shook her head. "I was just wondering how many other billionaires take the time to cook for themselves."

Giacomo grinned and kissed her. "I wasn't always a billionaire. Some things I couldn't give up. Back in Italy, we would always cook together, then at college, Lando and Carmel and I were known as the 'Gourmet Geeks.' I missed that until you. When Tara and I were dating, she would never entertain the idea of eating in. Having said that, she didn't entertain the idea of 'eating' that often either."

Norah shuddered. "I could never starve myself for work."

Giacomo smiled at her. "Glad to hear it. Although you could easily be a model."

"Boring."

"Quite."

She nudged his butt playfully with her foot. "I'm more than my looks."

"You don't have to tell me, Bella. I know that. Though I do think you are the most beautiful woman in the world, inside and out."

He said it so matter-of-factly, but tears sprang into her eyes. "What a lovely thing to say. Thank you."

"I mean it." He grinned wickedly then. "And not just because I want to get in your pants later."

She laughed. "It's working though."

AFTER DINNER, they sat in the living room, enjoying their evening and listening to the sultry tones of Billie Holiday playing on Giacomo's state-of-the-art stereo system. Norah lay with her head resting on Giacomo's lap and he stroked her hair.

"Bella?" He said, after they had enjoyed a comfortable silence for a while. She turned to look at him and he smiled down at her. "Ti amo."

"Ti amo, Giacomo."

"I've never been happier than in this moment with you."

She smiled and sat up, pressing her lips to his. "Me neither. You are my world, Giacomo."

He slid his fingers into her hair as they kissed tenderly at first, then as the heat between them increased, he gathered her into his arms and lay her back on the couch, covering her body with his. Pushing up her skirt, he pulled her panties off as she freed his cock from his underwear, stroking her hands up and down its length. Giacomo caressed her clit, feeling her sex swell and dampen for him, then as he pushed into her, he gazed down at her.

"I want you for all time, Norah Reddy. For all time. Marry me. Sposami ...be mine."

As they began to move together, Norah nodded, smiling through her tears. "Yes ...yes, Giacomo Conti. I will marry you..."

His smile made her weak, but she kissed him deeply as he began to thrust harder inside her in his joy, her fingers digging into his back as they made love.

Before long, they were naked and crying out the other's name as they came, then Giacomo carried her to their bed and they began again, wrapped up in each other. Giacomo looked down at her. "Remember when we said we ought to try some fun toys?"

Norah smiled, her eyes alive with desire. "I do."

"I took the liberty ..." He reached under the bed and brought out a box. "...of purchasing a few things to get started. Things we can use on each other."

Norah took the items out one by one, feeling herself get more and more turned on. Giacomo had chosen well—nothing too extreme. Nipple clamps, warming lube, bindings, dildos ... even a strap-on. She looked surprised. "Really?"

"Really." He kissed her. "Why should I be the only one to get to do that? We're a partnership, il mio amore. I do have something that, if you wouldn't mind, I would die to see you in." He lifted a body harness out of the box. Its dark red, supple leather was buttery soft. Giacomo looked at her, his eyes full of wanton desire. "May I?"

Norah smiled. "Please."

The soft leather crisscrossed her body, her breasts, and her belly, framing her navel before sweeping between her legs and over her buttocks. Giacomo sighed.

"God ...it was made for you." He slipped his hand between her legs. "You are turned on, yes?"

Norah shivered as his fingers touched her ultra-sensitive clit. "God, yes ...touch me like that ...god ..."

Giacomo smiled and lay her back on the bed, kissing her lips. "I'll tighten it now slightly." He pulled on the ends and the leather bit into her soft flesh. Giacomo's face was buried in her belly, his tongue rimming her navel. Norah moaned with desire. "Your turn now. What would you like me to do?"

His lips were against hers and she smiled. "I want to watch you bring yourself off. I want you to cum on my skin."

Giacomo chuckled. "Your wish, mio caro." He sat back on his haunches and fisted the root of his cock. "Bella, one last thing ... may I bind your hands?"

She nodded eagerly and he took a silk tie from the box and bound her hands loosely in front of her. They were both shivering with excitement now as Giacomo stroked the length of his cock, his eyes taking in the sight of her helpless in front of him. With his free hand, he stroked her clit, feeling it harden under his touch. "God, you're so beautiful ..." He said as they both began to pant. "I'm going to cum on your belly, then, my darling Norah, I'm going to fuck you so hard, so deep ..."

As he reached his peak, his seed shot out onto her dusky skin and Norah came at the sight of him, her clit almost unbearably responsive now. He didn't give her time to recover; he thrust his still rock-hard cock deep into her sodden cunt, ramming his hips hard against hers. He untied her hands and pinned them above her head as they moved together, the entire bed shaking and the headboard rattling loudly against the wall such was the force of his thrusts.

For Norah, it was a revelation, and she knew she would try anything with him ...her fiancé. He was so deep inside her that she could feel it in her belly and she came quickly, shaking like a leaf and gasping for air as his cock pumped sticky, creamy semen deep inside her. The leather bit into her skin painfully, but she loved the sting of it, the restraint, and the feeling that she was utterly at his mercy. She had never had a night like it.

Eventually, even they were exhausted. As they lay facing each other, Norah pressed her lips to his. "I'm yours forever, Giacomo. I can't wait to be your wife."

Giacomo smiled and she could see the depth of his joy in his beautiful eyes. "You are all I will ever want, il mio amore."

They fell asleep at last, wrapped in each other, limbs tangled, lips almost touching, and slept until morning.

CHAPTER TWELVE

Zulika looked at her with suspicion as soon as she walked through the door to the bookstore the next morning. Fred was due to start her first day at ten o'clock, but Zulika was still surprised to see her friend downstairs. Norah was singing softly to herself, her mahogany hair gathered up into a messy bun at the nape of her neck, her moves dance-like as she swept the floor. Zulika stood and watched her for a few minutes, a slow smile spreading across her face. Norah glanced up and saw her. Zulika stuck her tongue in the side of her cheek. "It's been a while since you did that."

Norah's eyebrows shot up. "Did what?"

"Sing to yourself. You always used to when we were at college. Sometimes you'd work your way through Pearl Jam's whole back catalog without even noticing. It made me laugh because you'd sing one line from each song and then move onto something else. Even Lucian liked it. He used to say it was one of his favorite thing about you."

Norah thought about it. "Huh. And I haven't been doing that?"

"Nope. Not for years. And then just lately, you started again." Zulika grinned.

Norah shrugged, smirked and started singing again. Zulika's eyes narrowed.

"Why are you radiant?"

Norah tried not to grin. "No idea what you're talking about." She hid her face, giggling to herself. She pretended to get something from under the counter. This would be fun. The truth was that she hadn't stopped smiling since Giacomo's proposal.

Zulika wasn't fooled. She hooked a finger into the back of Norah's t-shirt and pulled her friend up so she could see her face. Norah tried to keep her face blank, her eyes wide with innocence.

Zulika started to grin. "Yes, you do. You're glowing." She gasped. 'He hasn't gone and done it, has he?"

"Nope, no idea what you're burbling about." Norah tried to step around her, but Zulika moved too. They danced around each other until they both burst out laughing. Zulika grabbed her friend by the shoulders and made her look her in the eye.

"Has he? Has he proposed?"

"That information is not available at this time," Norah intoned, but she couldn't help smiling. Zulika squealed and hugged her.

"I knew it! Whoop!" She ran around the bookshop, waving her hands around her head.

Norah shook her head, grinning. "You loon."

Zulika stopped, still smiling. "Seriously, though, I'm so happy for you. Congratulations."

"Thank you, Zul. You don't think it's too fast, do you?"

"Hell, no. Not for you two. You belong together."

Norah smiled. "I think so too. Anyway, how are you?"

"I'm good. I actually went out for my first run this morning. Only did a couple of blocks, but it felt good."

"That's amazing, Zul …don't push yourself too hard, though."

Zulika rolled her eyes. "You sound like Lando. I'm fine."

NORAH WAITED until Fred came in and got settled, then excused herself to go up to her office. She flicked her laptop on and went to make a pot of coffee while she waited for it to boot up. Maybe I should invest in a new one, she thought as she waited for it. But she loved her trusty old laptop—even if Zulika, Giacomo, and Lando made fun of it.

"It is Methuselah," Zulika had teased her. "It doesn't have pixels, it has stone tablets."

Norah was grinning to herself as her email folder popped up. Her smile faded when she clicked on the first one. "Oh, no."

It was the cosmetics company she had been hired by, with a practically word-for-word copy of the letter she'd received the previous day. She was fired. Again.

"Fuck," she breathed. What the hell was going on?

Worse was to come. Three more clients had sent letters too, ending their contracts, each expressing their apologies but not giving her a reason for withdrawing their offers. Norah felt tears prick her eyes and she pulled her phone out and called Giacomo.

He sounded angry. "What the hell is their problem?"

"I honestly can't tell you, baby. I don't think I did anything wrong. My commission was lower than average, I offered to do extra work for them. I just don't get it."

"Are you okay, Bella?"

She sighed. "Yes, just disappointed. I feel like …god, I don't know … that my name has been sullied by this. I really hope not. I've worked too hard for this."

"You have. Look, Bella, there's plenty of work to do here …I'll send a car for you."

It was on the tip of her tongue to refuse, but instead, she found herself agreeing. She hid her upset from Zulika and Fred, and an hour later she was being driven out to Mountain View. Giacomo met her at the entrance, kissing her hello.

"I'm sorry, Bella."

She shook her head, wanting to cry. "It's Okayay. I just wished I knew why."

GIACOMO CALLED in some favors with some contacts, but everyone was closed-lipped. It wasn't until a few days later that they got their answer. An anonymous source at the cosmetics company sent Giacomo an image with the cryptic message: I think this will answer your question.

It was a mock-up of the campaign Norah had been set to work on, launching the brand's new line. Front and center of the photograph mock-up, in all her long-legged, icy blonde beauty …Tara.

Norah groaned and put her head on the desk. Giacomo cursed in Italian. He put his hand on Norah's hair. "Bella, I will sort this out. I promise."

Norah wanted to argue, but knew that Giacomo would have more luck than she in this area. He had the reputation and the status. Tara was an international supermodel. Who was this interloper, Norah Reddy? If a brand could get the unattainable Tara Hubert to front their campaign in return for dumping a newcomer, why wouldn't they?

"How did she know? How did she know who I was working with?"

Giacomo had no answer for her. "I will find out, mio caro. I promise you."

. . .

Seven o'clock and the bottle of sleeping pills just sat there, tempting her. Zulika sat on the kitchen counter, mindlessly munching an apple. The apartment was too quiet and too dark. Maybe running this morning had been a mistake. Her doctor had switched her medication and she was getting used to the new nausea, but it was distracting. Three days of taking the tablets had left her queasy and light-headed. Yes, they knocked her right out, but ... she went to the hallway to grab the phone and stopped. She picked up the photo of the four of them: Orlando, Norah, Giacomo, and herself. Happy. Happier, she corrected. Not perfect. She sighed and placed the photo face down. She took the phone into the living room and curled up in the armchair. Dialing, she waited for an answer.

'Hello?'

'Hey,' she smiled into the phone. "What are you doing this evening?'

Tara Hubert left dinner, and her date, at the restaurant and waited outside for the valet to bring her car around. As she slid into the driver's seat, she started the engine and moved off, but then screeched to a halt as Giacomo leaned forward from the backseat. Tara clutched her chest, her heart banging against her ribs. "What the fuck are you doing, Giacomo?"

His smile was chilling. "Oh, no. You first, Tara. What the fuck are you doing? Sabotaging Norah's career? I won't stand for it."

Tara smiled nastily. "Oh, you won't? And what exactly are you going to do about it?"

Giacomo met her eyes without saying a word and Tara quelled at the anger in them. She looked away. "So, she has to send you to fight her battles? Impressive."

"Tara, I would advise you not to test me. If you have a problem with me, fine. We will have to come to some sort of resolution. But Norah is off limits."

Tara sneered. "I'm just doing my job, Giacomo. Can I help it if they don't want some half-baked artist on their campaign?"

"I'm warning you, Tara."

She turned in her seat. "Get out of my car, Giacomo ...unless you want me to drive you back to my apartment. I'm sure we can come to some kind of agreement there."

Giacomo's nose turned up. "You need to come to terms with the fact I'm never coming back to you, Tara. Ever. That boat has sailed a long time ago now. I'm off the market for good. Norah and I will be married very soon."

Tara flinched at his words, pain shooting through her. "Well, what a fucking heart-warming Cinderella story that'll be."

"Do you understand me, Tara?"

"Get out of my car, Giacomo, before I scream."

"My pleasure. Goodbye, Tara." And he was gone.

Tara sat for a few minutes, brooding. Giacomo Conti, married. After how many months? Six? And yet in five years with Tara, he hadn't even mentioned it once.

Fuck you, Giacomo. And fuck your beautiful fiancée.

You won't get away with this.

ZULIKA TOUCHED her glass to Orlando's and grinned at him. "I hope I didn't cause you too much trouble by inviting you out tonight."

They were seated in a little burger joint downtown, tall glasses of soda in front of them, waiting for their food. Orlando shook his head, smiling. "You saved me from an evening of twiddling my thumbs. Ferma's at a sleepover with one of her friends—the first one since her mom died, and honestly, I had no idea how to entertain myself again. I miss your company in the evenings."

"And I, yours. I still think I needed to move back home and get independent, but yeah, some nights, I miss just looking over at you and saying some random factoid."

Orlando laughed. "Ah, yes, your encyclopedic knowledge of ...everything."

"Jealous."

He laughed again. "Always. How's the new girl working out at the store?"

"Fred? She's fantastic. I'm sure she's some kind of Pied Piper of Books—our sales have gone through the roof."

They chatted easily throughout their meal, both groaning afterward that their bellies were full. They walked down to the Golden Gate bridge and leaning against the railing, looking out at the boats on the Bay, then Orlando asked her if she'd like to come back to his house for a drink.

"Sure thing," she said and he grinned

"Race you."

"Oh, ha ha," she grimaced, rubbing her full belly, "I actually think that burger might have killed me."

"Fatty."

"Hey!" She giggled and they teased each other mercilessly as they walked to find a cab.

At home, she breathed in the comforting smell of the place: books, records, the faint hint of breakfast cereal, and Orlando's woodsy, clean scent. When they had settled on the couches, Orlando passed her a bottle of beer and they sat back.

"When I was sick, I never told you how much of a comfort being here with you and Ferma was."

Orlando smiled. "You did. You said it all the time."

Zulika chuckled. "I guess I did ...but did you ever realize how much it meant to me? You and Ferma were a lifeline. I don't know if my recovery would have gone so well."

Orlando looked a little uncomfortable. "Well, now, I'm sure if you had told Norah at the start ..."

"Oh, I know. But it didn't work out like that. You will never know how glad I was to run into you at the hospital, that day."

She suddenly realized what she'd said and was horrified. "God, Lando, I mean ...Jesus. Me and my big mouth. I'm so sorry."

You idiot, she berated herself. Did you really just say you were glad he was at the hospital to pick up his dead wife's things? His murdered wife? Idiot. Idiot. Idiot.

Orlando put his hand over hers. "Zulika, chill. I know what you meant. I'm glad I was there for you too."

He left his hand on hers and Zulika could not help winding her fingers through his. She stared at their conjoined hands for a long moment and then looked up. She met Orlando's curious gaze and then, so, so naturally, their lips met. His mouth was soft and his lips gentle. Zulika found a myriad of sensations flooding through her as they kissed.

"Lando?" She whispered, but he shook his head.

"Don't say anything. Just ..."

He slid his arms around her and pulled her close, kissing her deeply, passionately. Zulika found her arms curling around his neck, her fingers tangling in his black hair.

Orlando moved her onto her back, his hands pushing up her shirt. Zulika, breathless, tugged his t-shirt over his head and ran her hands over the hard muscles of his chest. He was solidly built, his shoulders broad and his arms thickly muscled. As they stripped, she couldn't help but admire the rest of him—his long legs, powerful thighs, and thick, proud cock.

As he covered her body with his, Zulika felt as if she were dreaming, and when his cock slid into her, she gasped at the pain mixed with such heady pleasure she thought she might pass out. They made love tenderly and slowly, exploring each other's bodies. Orlando braced his hands on either side of her, gazing down at her as he began to thrust harder and deeper, and Zulika was lost, almost delirious with pleasure.

As she came, she heard him groan out her name again and again with such tenderness that she almost wept. "I love you so much, Lando. So, so much."

But as he caught his breath, Zulika saw the change come over his face. Oh no, no, not this, please ...

Guilt.

He withdrew from her, sitting up. Zulika pushed herself up, reaching for him, but he flinched away. He turned back to her almost immediately, but the damage was done. Zulika covered her naked breasts, mortified.

"I'm so sorry," he said, his voice barely a whisper. "I can't. Not ...in her house ..."

Zulika felt hot tears of shame flood down her cheeks, but she nodded. "I understand. I'll go ..."

She started to pull her clothes on, but Lando reached for her. "I'm sorry, Zul. Please believe me when I say it is me, not you."

God. She shook her head, unable to speak.

He walked her to the door. "Let me call you a cab."

She shook her head. "No, I need the air."

She turned to go, but he pulled her back into his arms. Leaning his forehead against hers, she could feel his tears dripping onto her face. "I'm so sorry, Zul ...I want to be able to love you, to be free to love you ...I'm just not there yet."

She kissed him softly. "It's okay."

But as she ran into the night, down his street, she knew it wasn't Okay. She debated calling a cab, but she didn't want to be around anyone. The bookstore was only a couple of blocks.

She'd stay there tonight, alone. Somewhere she could collect herself.

Somewhere she could cry her heart out and no-one would hear her.

Tara straddled him and rode his cock impatiently, needing him to come fast and hard. She needed the ego boost—and she needed Lucian to help her with the next part of her plan.

Which was why she was fucking him again; the only reason. He had long since started to revolt her, but now, with his cock buried deep inside her cunt, she knew she had all the power over him she needed.

Because soon, very soon she was going to need him to kill his ex-girlfriend.

"Zulika. Zulika. Zulika." A poke in the ribs. "Boss. Wake up."

Zulika opened her eyes to see Fred leaning over her, at once amused and annoyed. The sun was streaming in from the windows. Fred had obviously opened the blinds before she'd seen Zulika. Zulika blinked a few times, her head a fuzzy whirl. She sat up, clutching the throw to her naked body.

"Jeez. What time is it?"

"Nine a.m. What on earth are you doing in here?"

Zulika stood, wrapping the blanket around her tightly. "Nine a.m.? Damn, I must have been tired."

"Why are you asleep on the couches anyway? You know you have a bed at home, right?"

"I couldn't be bothered to go home." Zulika was gathering up her clothes. She could have sworn she'd left her underwear on, but now she found it folded neatly on top of her jeans and t-shirt. Her limbs felt strange—sore as if she's been lifting weights. "I need to take a shower."

Fred frowned. "You could have crashed on my couch, you know. And if you're going to be buck naked, you might want to make sure the door's locked. The back door was open."

Zulika stopped. "What?"

Fred nodded. "Yep. Unless ..." Fred grinned wickedly. "You were expecting company?"

Zulika rolled her eyes. "Behave yourself."

Fred threw her a grin. "Go clean yourself up, you shameless hussy. I'll let the screaming hoards in. Wait ..." She stopped Zulika and peered at her, frowning. "How'd you get that?" She poked at Zulika's neck and Zulika winced.

"What is it?" She went out to the back room and looked in the mirror.

"You've got a hickey." Fred stood watching her, arms folded across her chest.

"Whatever." Zulika let her hair drop, shrugged, and headed upstairs. Her eyes stung and she sighed when she saw her red eyes and puffy cheeks. She had a terrible pain in her chest, but she knew it wasn't anything physical. Torturing herself, she checked her phone for messages. None.

Oh god. What had she been thinking? Had she ruined her friendship with Orlando because of a one night stand? The thought of never seeing him again was breaking her heart, but seeing him would be even harder.

Help me, I don't know what to do.

She flicked to the keypad on her phone and called the one person she knew she could talk to.

Norah.

. . .

Norah took one look at Zulika's face and sent her home. "I'll finish out the day with Fred, then come to you. I'll tell Giacomo I won't be home tonight."

Zulika dragged herself home and fell into bed to sleep until Norah came over. As she was falling asleep, the tears came, and she sobbed again, trying to tell herself that it shouldn't make such a big difference. So she had a one night stand with her friend, her recently-bereaved friend, and he'd freaked out. He hadn't said she disgusted him, or that he didn't want her. He just felt guilty.

Which was bad enough, because so did Zulika. Not just because of Carmel. Not just because of her friend, but because, for Zulika, last night had been more than sex—more than just a one night stand.

It had been her first time. And for a second, it seemed like it had been the perfect way to say goodbye to her long-held virginity. And it had. It had been perfect. Until it wasn't.

She rolled over onto her front and buried her tears in her pillow.

CHAPTER THIRTEEN

Giacomo knew that Norah was with Zulika, so he decided to go see his god-daughter and Orlando. Ferma was excited; Norah had already asked her to be her flower-girl and as soon as Giacomo arrived, she was showing him the sketches she had made of her dream dress.

"I would show you the ones I did of Auntie Norah," she told him seriously, "But you're not supposed to see her dress and if she picks one of them, then that's bad luck."

"I understand," he said in a grave voice, then winked at Lando. His friend looked tired. "Youokay, man?"

Lando mouthed, "Later," at him and Giacomo nodded. After take-out pizza, Ferma went to bed, the two men sat outside with cold beers, and Lando told him about his night with Zulika.

Giacomo listened, then patted his friend's back. "Lando, I have to say, it's not the biggest surprise."

"It isn't?"

Giacomo shrugged. "Anyone can see you two are crazy about each other."

Orlando groaned, dropping his head into his hands. "That's

just it. Carmel hasn't even been gone a year. How could I fall for someone else so quickly?"

"Give yourself a break, Lando. Did you mean to fall in love again? No. Are you disrespecting Carmel's memory? Hell, no. She's up there, cheering you on. You know how much Carmel and Zulika liked each other. Ferma adores her. No one expects you to be a monk."

Orlando rubbed his eyes and sighed. "I promised I wouldn't get involved with anyone until I got closure for myself. For Ferma. Until we know who killed Carmel and why ..."

"Lando, listen to me." Giacomo's voice was serious. "Here's the brutal truth; we may never know. I'm sorry if that sounds harsh. Whether it was someone targeting Carmel or just a random psychopath ...we might never know. You cannot put your life on hold for that."

Orlando said nothing, staring out unseeingly at the backyard. Giacomo swigged his beer.

"Can I ask you something?"

"Of course, mio fratello."

Orlando looked him and Giacomo winced at the pain in his eyes. "What if something happened to Norah, then less than a year later you realized ...I'm in love with this whole new person? How would you feel?"

Giacomo hesitated and then nodded. "I understand."

"No, tell me. How would you feel? If someone murdered Norah, if someone shot her six times when she was carrying your child, if someone ended her life in cold blood ..."

"Stop." Giacomo felt sick. Even though he knew Orlando was really talking to himself now, the images he was conjuring were making Giacomo's heart beat so hard against his ribs that it was painful.

Orlando dropped his head into his hands and Giacomo could see his shoulders shaking.

"Lando ...stop torturing yourself. It happened."

"Giacomo, what if, by being careless, I've ruined Zulika's life and my life? I want my friend back, but I've hurt her. I know I have."

Giacomo hugged his friend in his distress. "Lando, I promise. You will get through this. It's not an impossible situation."

ORLANDO WALKED SLOWLY over and pushed the door open. The Anthology was empty of customers. Norah looked up at him and he raised his eyebrows at her. She grinned and wandered out to the back room. Orlando walked to the counter and saw Norah push an equally confused Zulika into the store. Norah shut the door behind her, leaving them alone. Orlando braced himself, but was wrong-footed when Zulika gave him a shy smile.

"Hi." She blushed a little.

"Hey." He shook himself and smiled back. "You okay?"

She nodded and poured out coffee for him. Orlando sat down, not wanting the spell to break, but not knowing what to say. Zulika seemed at a loss too.

"Zul– "

"We have new cupcakes. Pumpkin."

He laughed and a moment later she grinned. "Sorry. That was the lamest conversation opener ever."

"Nope. Nope. Pumpkin cupcakes. Way early for Halloween though."

"Test run."

"Ah, so I'm your guinea pig?" He picked one up and peeled the paper back.

"Yep. I was going to say it's because of your fine palette, but really it's because you'll eat anything." She grinned at him, relaxing. Orlando nodded.

"Pretty much." He bit into the cake and chewed. "It's good."

She narrowed her eyes at him. "Your face is saying something else entirely."

Orlando shrugged and grinned, putting the other half of the cake down. "You got me. Sorry, sweetheart, they're not great."

She grinned. "Yeah, that's what Norah and I thought."

Orlando's eyes widened. "Ah, so, you just thought you'd have a little fun with me, then?"

"Yep." She was laughing at him now, looking like his Zulika rather than the stressed-out wraith of the last few days. "Why waste some perfectly good, or as the case may be, not so good cupcakes?"

"Ha ha ha." But he grinned. "Seriously, you okay?"

She nodded. "Yeah. Getting there. You?"

"Same. Look—"

"Don't say anything. Not yet. Let's just enjoy ..." She gestured around the both of them.

"You got it."

She gave him a grateful smile. "So, not pumpkin. I need ideas for Halloween food. We're going to have a kid's party here. Fred's idea. Maybe Ferma could come?"

He smiled at her. "I think I can guarantee she will."

"Good." Zulika smiled, her body relaxing. "So, any ideas?"

Orlando stroked his chin, pretending to ponder. "Ghosts on Toast. Ghost Toast. It's a winner."

She nodded, pretending to consider it seriously. "Just so happens, they've got a special on ghosts at the market."

Orlando clicked his tongue and gave her the finger pistols. She grinned and refilled his cup. "You are so silly."

He chuckled. "Always happy to help, ma'am." He looked around. "Quiet in here today."

Zulika nodded. "It's hot outside. Everyone is at the beach."

Orlando smiled at her. "Zul, we can't ignore what happened

between us. For what it's worth ...I don't regret the act. I certainly don't regret it was with you. I just got ..."

"Freaked out." He nodded and she smiled. "Me too. Lando ... would it make you feel better if I said it was pretty momentous for me too? Lando ...it was my first time."

For a second he thought he hadn't heard her right. "Excuse me?"

Zulika flushed red, but she gave a soft laugh. "That's usually the reaction. I was a virgin, Lando."

Orlando realized he was gaping at her, then he shut his mouth. "Oh, Zul ..."

"It's okay. I'm glad I waited. I'm glad, even with the circumstances, that it was you."

Orlando hesitated for a moment, then got up and came around the counter. He pulled her into his arms and hugged her. "I don't know what to say."

She leaned into him, her face buried in his chest. "Don't say anything. Let's just stay like this for a moment."

IN THE BACK ROOM, Norah scribbled a note telling Zulika she was going out to lunch with Giacomo, then she skipped out. Giacomo was just pulling the car up to the curb and smiling. She got in and kissed him hello.

"You taste so good," she murmured against his lips,,and he laughed.

"Are you hungry, mio caro?"

She grinned, nuzzling his neck. "Not for food, no."

"Insatiable."

"You betcha. Take me somewhere and fuck me, Conti."

Giacomo grinned as he started the car. "You're horny today, il mio amore?"

"For you, every day." She took his hand and slid it under her dress, laughing as his eyebrows shot up when he encountered bare flesh.

"Jesus, Norah ..." He was grinning widely as he began to caress her clit. She grinned and put her hand over his cock.

"Take me to Baker Beach ...you know where ..."

She was pretty sure they got there in record time, but still, by the time he parked the car, they were both so worked up that he fucked her there in the back seat of his car, going down on her first hungrily, then slamming his cock so deep into her that she screamed with pleasure.

"God, you make me so hot, Bella," he growled as he pushed her legs further apart.

They almost got caught twice, reducing them to giggles, but after two orgasms, Norah sighed happily. "I love you, Giacomo Conti. You make we want to do things I've never even considered."

He started the car, his dark curls wild and his face flushed, but he grinned. "Just think of all the things we haven't done yet. I'm thinking of taking you back to my island again—and maybe bringing some new stuff we could have fun with. You could be naked all day, every day. That's my dream."

She stroked the hair over his ear as he drove her to a small trattoria for something to eat. "And so could you. That's my dream. Oh, that reminds me." She delved into her purse and retrieved the panties she had slipped off earlier. "I can't go commando while we eat."

He was still laughing when they walked hand-in-hand into the restaurant.

ORLANDO GOT UP RELUCTANTLY, pondering whether to call and get the sitter to go pick Ferma up from school. He had been in the Anthology all day now, talking to Zulika and Norah, helping out, and laughing and joking with the customers. Zulika touched his arm. "You okay?"

"Yep. Just thinking about Ferma."

Norah grinned. "Why don't you two go pick her up?" She winked at Zulika and disappeared into the back.

Orlando nodded, looking at Zulika. "Walk with me?"

She smiled up at him. "Aren't you tired? We have been working you hard all day."

"It was fun."

She laughed. "Try doing it all day, every day."

"Don't give me that. You love it."

She nodded. "Yeah, I do." She took the pumpkin cupcakes, untouched since that morning, and dumped them in the trash. "Funny we didn't sell any more of these. It's almost as if someone were telling the customers how bad they were." She stuck her tongue out at Orlando, who grinned.

"What do you say to grabbing supper with Ferma and me?"

She looked away, hesitated, then nodded. "Yes, thank you. I would love that."

He walked around the counter, hesitated, but then hugged her. She leaned against him for a second before pulling away. She smiled. He looked down at her.

"Wish I could say everything I want to you. Wish that very much."

She nodded. "Me too. But best not. Makes it harder."

"Yeah. I know. We both need time."

"We do. Now, let's go get Ferma."

As they walked out of the store, Orlando's stride was lighter. His heartache was easing. Friends. Still family. It helped a lot.

SIX MONTHS. Six months in the planning and it all came down to a few minutes today. Lucian looked at Tara as they sat in the car and she smiled at him. "Don't look so worried. It's going to be fine."

He hoped so.

AFTER ORLANDO and Zulika had left, Norah watched them walk to the corner of the street and smiled to herself. Was this a good sign? She was just tidying the store when she heard the knock on the back door. Distracted, she forgot to check who it was. As she opened it and, to her dismay, saw it was Lucian, she tried to close it again, but he kicked it in, sending her flying back and crashing to the floor. He was on her then, pinning her hands down and sitting on her legs so she couldn't move or run.

"I just want to talk, Norah. Talk. Just hear me out."

"Motherfucker!" She struggled with him, half-crazed, "Let me go. Let me go."

Lucian forced his mouth onto hers to quiet her and she started to sob.

"For fuck's sake, just listen to me for a few minutes, then I'll be gone," he lied. Still growling, Norah stared up at him.

"Nothing you could say is of any interest to me, you psycho."

He punched her in the stomach and she recoiled, the wind knocked out of her. "Now, I didn't want to do that, Norah, but you won't behave yourself."

She was gasping for air as he got up and she curled herself into a ball for a second before scrambling to her feet and backing away from him.

Lucian held his hands up. "I just want to talk about your impending wedding. I can't let you marry that man, Norah. I just can't. You belong to me."

"I don't belong to anyone!" She screamed at him, "I'm not a fucking possession. You don't get to tell me how to run my life, you piece of shit."

Lucian leaped at her, his anger exploding as he picked her up and threw her across the room, shattering the window to the back room. Covered in glass, Norah clambered to her feet, ready to fight back, but he was too quick and too brutal. He slammed his fist into her belly again and again.

Norah cried out, but Lucian, half-crazed with rage, didn't stop. He beat her to the floor, punching her in the temple and kicking her viciously in the stomach. "Fucking bitch whore! You ruined my life!"

Blood poured from the cuts and gashes on Norah's body, but it only spurred Lucian to greater violence. Only when he noticed that Norah had stopped moving did he step back, breathing heavily. God …was she dead? He dropped to his knees and felt her throat, searching for a pulse.

"Norah?"

Alive. Her breathing was ragged, hitching. Suddenly sense flooded back into Lucian's fevered mind and he reeled away from her. What have I done?

Breathing deeply, he pulled his phone out, finding it slipped through his fingers. He saw the blood on his hands. "Oh god … Tara? Tara, god, I'm at the bookstore …I think … I think I fucked up. Help me."

"What do you want me to do?"

She sounded bored and Lucian lost it. "I just beat the crap out of my ex-girlfriend! Help me, you nasty little cunt! You wanted me to come see her. You must have known what would happen."

Tara sighed. "Is she dead?"

"No, she's not fucking dead." Lucian was screaming now.

"Calm down, Lucian. It's obvious what you need to do. You can't leave her like that; she'll lead the police right to you."

"What are you telling me to do?"

"Kill her." Tara's voice was cold and flat. Lucian couldn't help but groan.

"I can't kill her, Tara. ?For fuck's sake."

"Yes, you can. There's a kitchen in that hole of a bookstore, right? Find a knife and cut her throat. Or, if it's blunt, stick it in her gut a few times. That should do it. Make it look like a robbery."

Lucian felt the sweat begin to pool on the back of his neck. Could he? Could he kill Norah in cold blood like that? His legs were moving as of their own accord. He walked into the kitchen and pulled open some drawers. "There's a knife."

"Do it. Then this is all over for everyone."

Lucian took up the blade, barely registering what he was doing, and went back out to his unconscious ex-girlfriend. The knife was a dinner knife, almost blunt, so he pushed up Norah's top and pressed the tip against her skin. His hand tightened around the handle and he jabbed it once, quickly. It didn't even break the skin.

"It's too blunt."

"Do it from a height. Really slam it into her." Jesus. Tara was psychotic. Lucian dropped the blade. If only he hadn't waited … he could have killed Norah that day when she used her knee on him. That day he was angry enough. That day he had had a sharp enough weapon with him. Except …could he really go through with it? Kill another person? Kill his Norah? After all he had threatened and had imagined doing—he couldn't go through with it.

"Is it done? Is she dead?"

Lucian said nothing for a moment, then he gritted his teeth. "She's dead. I did what you said."

He heard Tara heave a sigh of relief. "Thank fuck. Now get out of there and don't contact me for a few days. I'll call you."

Lucian hung up the phone, then stared down at his very

much alive ex-lover. She was drenched in blood, with cuts from the window and his fist, her lips split, and a wide gash at her hairline. Blood was pooling beneath her. He knew what he had to do now ...it was just a matter of how.

GIACOMO, having done no work all afternoon, was still smiling from their lunchtime escapade together as he pulled up at the bookstore. He got out, knowing she might be upstairs working, and went around the back.

He stopped. The back door was ajar; Norah would never, ever leave it like that. The window was smashed. No, god, no, please ...

Taking out his handkerchief, he used it to push the door open and saw the devastation inside. Broken glass, smashed furniture, and blood everywhere.

Giacomo couldn't breathe. Something bad had happened here. Something very bad and the worst of it was obvious.

Norah was gone ...

Zulika shot an agonized glance at Orlando, who himself looked pale and shocked. Giacomo sat with his head in his hands as the police moved around them, gathering evidence and studying the chaos of the Anthology's back room. Zulika kept seeing the blood, the smashed glass, and the debris of what had to be a violent and brutal fight.

Norah was gone. Was she dead? Zulika had no doubt that Lucian was behind this horror; Giacomo had told the police as much. He looked broken. "I should never have let her out of my sight."

Zulika hugged him. "You know Norah would have hated that. One of the reasons she loves you is that you don't control her and you don't try and tell her what to do. This is not your fault, Giacomo."

"Then why do I feel like it is?" He closed his eyes and drew in a deep breath. "The one bright thing is ...I feel she is still alive. I know it. He took her because he wanted her, not because ...not to hide her ..."

He couldn't finish that sentence and Zulika nodded. "That's a good thing to cling to, Giacomo."

Orlando cleared his throat. "The police are asking us to come to the station, answer some questions, and help with the search."

Giacomo looked up at his friend. "Good. I've already got my security out and looking ...Mio Dio..."

Zulika saw him staring down at the pool of blood on the floor. "He beat her," he whispered. "He hurt her."

He sounded so desolate that Zulika felt tears drop down her face and she began to cry.

THE FIRST THING she registered was the smell. Musty sheets and the sharp stench of industrial cleaner. The sound. A television. Norah opened her eyes. She lay on a bed, her left hand handcuffed to the frame. Every part of her body hurt, her vision was blurry, and her eyes were stinging. She retched at the stench of the room and then someone hovered into view.

"Don't throw up. You're gagged. You'll drown in your own vomit."

Lucian. She tried to stretch her mouth free from the duct tape covering it, glaring at him and growling as best she could. Lucian laughed.

"I wouldn't bother, Norah. No-one is going to hear you out here. Manager's an old buddy. No one knows you're here."

He stroked her face tenderly. "I had to take you with me, Norah. It was the only way to save you."

She bugged out her eyes at him in disbelief, then wished she hadn't. A headache screeched around her skull and she winced, closing her eyes. A few moments later, she felt a cold cloth against her forehead and felt some relief, despite herself. Lucian washed her face in cool water; she could hear him rinsing the cloth and when she opened her eyes, she could see a bowl of pinkish water. Blood.

"I'm sorry I got so rough, baby. I didn't mean it."

He was crazy. He was actually crazy. Norah felt the fear clenching at her stomach. Was he going to kill her? What had he meant by 'saving' her?

Lucian put the bowl of water down on the floor and looked at her. "Now, I'm going to take that gag off. You can scream and holler ...but no-one is out here and it'll just make me angry again. I don't want to hurt you, Norah, so don't make me."

He ripped off the duct tape in one fast motion and she gasped. She licked her dry lips and he held a cup of cold water to her mouth. She gulped it down gratefully, all the time deciding whether to scream or not.

Not. Lucian meant what he said and Norah knew she would have to be crafty to stand a chance of getting out of here alive.

"Why did you take me?"

Lucian sighed. "Because ...someone told me to kill you. I couldn't do it. And this ...person ...would have made me do it."

"Who?"

He didn't answer and Norah decided not to push it. Who would want her dead? She didn't think she had any enemies—not psychotic ones, anyway. The only person who had physically harmed her was right here and now he was telling her was 'saving' her? There was only one answer.

Lucian was insane.

Norah looked away from him. "Do you have any aspirin? My head is killing me."

Silently, he got up and went into the bathroom and Norah

used the opportunity to take in her surroundings. They were obviously in a sleazy motel—she didn't want to think about the counterpane she was lying on or what lurked in it. She gagged again gently, then shook herself. Concentrate. Her left arm was cuffed to the bed frame, but the cuffs were the kind you could get in an adult store—flimsy. She was pretty sure she could get out of them. Her stomach hurt the most and she pulled up her shirt and winced. Huge black and blue bruises covered her skin, along with the impression of a boot print.

Bastard. She ran her tongue over her dry lips and tasted blood. Lucian had really beaten her to a pulp. *How am I still alive?*

Don't ask that. The important thing is you are still alive. Now it's time to figure how to get away from him.

She knew Lucian and knew his fatal flaw. His arrogance and self-adoration. She would play up to it and seduce him into trusting her.

Lucian appeared with two aspirin and another cup of water. She swallowed the pills down gratefully and leaned back, closing her eyes. She felt his lips against hers and felt sick.

Kiss him. Start the process.

She couldn't bring herself to respond, but she didn't pull away. Lucian kissed her sore, tender mouth gently. "I love you so much, Norah."

She felt something cold press against her belly and when Lucian drew away, she saw it. The muzzle of the pistol was hard against her skin. Lucian smiled, but his eyes were cold.

"This is just a reminder, Norah. Don't fuck with me or I'll have to use this on you, and I really, really, don't think either of us wants that. I love you, baby, but I will shoot you dead if you try to run."

Norah felt cold at his words. This was really happening,

wasn't it? She waited until Lucian was asleep before she let the tears fall. Please let me see Giacomo again. Please.

She sobbed quietly until, just after midnight, she fell into an uneasy sleep.

GIACOMO MADE sure Norah's abduction was all over the news and that Lucian's name and image were flashed up everywhere. California State Police was on alert, and because of Giacomo's position and wealth, the FBI got involved.

After the statutory twenty-four hours had gone by, he sent an exhausted and drained Zulika home, telling Orlando to take care of her. In his apartment alone, Giacomo stared out at the city.

"Where are you, il mio amore?" He leaned his head against the window. In the other room, he could hear the FBI agents talking in low voices, but he had never felt more alone than now. He slumped into his chair, the chair where he and Norah would sit with her cradled in his arms, her long legs swung over the arm rest, and her lips against his neck. They'd even tried to have sex on the armchair one time, but had to give up, laughing when it became awkward and impossible. He could still see her smile now, and the way she'd wiped the tears of laughter from her eyes.

He had wrestled her playfully to the carpet, spreading her legs wide and seeking her clit with his tongue. God, the taste of her...

She had moaned and writhed under his touch, his mouth on her, and he'd given her two orgasms before she had moaned that she needed him inside her. His cock was almost painfully swollen and as he grinned down at her and pushed inside, her long sigh of pleasure sent his pulse racing. They moved together, their gazes locked on the other, each wanting to give as much pleasure to the other as possible. He'd pinned her hands to the carpet and she'd smiled at his dominance.

"I would do anything with you, my love," she whispered. "Anything you'd ever wanted to try, anything you dreamed about. Just ask."

"Right now, Principessa, all I can think about is how your silky cunt feels on my cock …"

Her breath had quickened at his coarseness and he had chuckled, beginning to thrust harder and longer with each stroke, wanting to be deep, deep inside her.

Giacomo choked back a sob. Could it be possible he might never see her smile again? No. Wherever you are, il mio amore, fight. He grabbed his car keys and headed out of the apartment, not knowing where he was going, just knowing that he could not, would not, ever stop looking for her.

CHAPTER FOURTEEN

Orlando had driven them both back to his home without asking her if she would like to be there. Zulika realized he knew how much she would need him around, especially if, god forbid, they got bad news.

The house was quiet when they arrived. "Where's Ferma?"

"At a friend's ...I called them and told them what was happening. They offered to throw an impromptu sleep-over."

Zulika sighed. "All this disruption in her young life."

"I know. Listen, sit. I'll make us some Irish coffees. I think we could both use the boost."

Zulika smiled at him. "That would be nice."

In the living room, she flicked on the television, turned to the news, and watched the reports of Norah's abduction. She wondered if Norah hadn't been the fiancée of billionaire Giacomo Conti, how much of this news would simply be buried. A half-Indian, half-African-American girl goes missing in big city. Would it even be reported? Zulika gritted her teeth. She knew the answer to that already.

"Why are you glaring at the television?" Orlando was back

with their coffee and giving her a quizzical, half-amused glance. She told him and he sighed.

"I hear ya. It's why I'm overprotective with Ferma. When I was a kid out in the projects, dozens went missing. Not a peep from the T.V. news. It was almost ...expected? Is that the right word?"

Zulika nodded. "Understood. I'm torn between being outraged that Norah is deemed important enough to report on because of who she's sleeping with and being glad that they are reporting on her, regardless of circumstances."

Orlando nodded, but said nothing. They sat in companionable silence, watching the news, listening to the same sound bites and interviews over and over, and not hearing any progress. Zulika got more agitated as 'experts' commented on Norah and Giacomo's relationship, Norah's past, and even at one point her fashion sense.

"What has that got to do with anything?" Zulika screeched at the television, then looked at Orlando, who was trying not to laugh at her indignation. He cracked and that set her off, laughter giving her blessed relief from the tension.

"God, why am I laughing?" She said eventually, "It's so inappropriate."

Orlando patted her leg. "You know what? Admittedly, I haven't known Norah that long, but I know she would be laughing too."

Zulika nodded, a pang of sadness hitting her. "She would." She was silent for a moment. "I can see her now ...wearing the latest in hostage chic ... God."

She was trying to make a joke, but she got choked.

"Deep breaths, Zul." Orlando's arm was around her shoulders. She leaned into him for comfort. "Try to think it'll all be okay. Believe it will be."

"I do believe," she said quietly." I believe in her. I believe in Norah."

Orlando pressed his lips against her temple. "Me too, kiddo. Me too."

LUCIAN WAITED until Norah fell asleep, then picked up his phone. Tara had been calling him all day, but he'd ignored it. He called her back now and as soon as she picked up, she was yelling at him.

"What the fuck, Lucian? Did you kill her or not? Tell me, please, that you dumped her body somewhere and you haven't been so stupid as to be keeping her alive somewhere?"

Lucian let her rant for a few minutes, then when she paused for breath, he spoke in a low, angry voice. "Listen to me, you little bitch ...who do you think you are? Norah, and what I do with or to her, is none of your concern. I got her away from Conti—isn't that what you wanted?"

He glanced back at Norah, asleep on the bed. She hadn't stirred during the call. "I'm going to disappear and take Norah with me."

"Oh, yes?" Tara laughed nastily, "Really? It'll be that easy, will it? From what I've seen of Norah Reddy, she's no pushover. Do you think she'll say, Why, yes, Lucian, seeing as you asked so nicely...you stupid, stupid man."

"Fuck you," Lucian shot back. "You don't know the history we have between us. We were meant to be together."

"Oh, please, spare me the Hallmark clichés. She's in love with Giacomo ...do you really want me to list all the ways that you don't begin to compare to him? Do yourself a favor, Lucian. Put a bullet in your ex-girlfriend and leave the state. You'll be better off. Where are you, anyway?"

Lucian smiled to himself. "Nowhere you'll find us. You think I'm going to tell you, psycho?"

"Fine. I'm sure the police will catch up with you anyway ...it's not like you give Mensa a run for their money, is it?"

Lucian ended the call with a growl. Fucking bitch. He turned and looked around at Norah. There were deep shadows under her eyes, bruises on her cheeks, and cuts and bruises on her lovely mouth. For a second, he felt shame. How could he have done this to her?

He crouched next to her and stroked the hair away from her face. "I'm sorry, beautiful."

His voice was only a whisper, but she opened her eyes and looked back at him. "Hi," he said tenderly. "Are you okay?"

Norah said nothing, but gave a small nod of her head before closing her eyes again. Lucian leaned in and pressed his lips to hers. No, Tara, I won't kill her. How can I when everything I have ever wanted is within my grasp? "I love you," he whispered. He lay down next to her, spooning her body. Slipping his arm around her waist, he stroked her belly through her t-shirt. Norah didn't react. Lucian closed his eyes and, as he fell asleep, he pretended that they were still like they used to be ...in love.

NORAH WASN'T okay at all. She wasn't in the region of being okay. She felt sick and light-headed, and her body ached, not just with fear and sadness, but with something she couldn't get a grip on. Where Lucian had kicked her, her stomach felt odd, as if something wasn't right inside of her. She could taste blood constantly and wondered if she was bleeding internally.

All of which meant ...she had no time. She had to figure out a way to get away from Lucian, and fast. She had to make him let his guard down. God, the thought at the back of her mind that kept sneaking forward—that she might have to seduce him to make him vulnerable. The thought made her want to vomit, but she told herself, anything to get away, to get back to Giacomo, back to salvation.

She had faked being asleep during the phone call and had listened to everything Lucian had said. She knew the other person had to be Tara. Who else could it be? Tara was the only person in the world she knew had a motive to want her ...gone. She still couldn't believe Tara would go so as to want her dead. Jesus. That had scared her more than Lucian. It was always more of a betrayal when a woman behaved like that, at least for Norah. It upset her to think someone of her own sex could want to kill her. God, how fucked up is that? she asked herself. Like you expect it from a man?

Yes. God, help her, but yes. How many things in life were off-limits to a woman because a man might kill her? Long walks at night. Not taking risks. Dressing how she wanted.

You're getting off the point, Reddy. But her mind was whirling with all sorts of messed up thoughts. She drew in a long breath and shifted out of Lucian's grasp. She hated that he had the gall to hold her like a lover, instead of her attacker or her kidnapper. To hold her like Giacomo did—to sully that memory. And, yes, the thought had occurred to her. She would kill Lucian if she could. If it meant being free of him. A plan began to form in her mind and for the rest of the night, she went over and over it ...distracting herself from the growing agony in her body and the feeling that her time was running out.

GIACOMO WAS IN HIS OFFICE, his security team around him being briefed by the FBI. As much as he wanted to find Norah himself, he had to admit that he didn't have the expertise needed to comb the city, the state, and the country, if needed.

"There's no way they'll get out of the country," The FBI team leader had told him. "We have notices up at every airport, border, and port. If his passport pings, we'll have him."

"What if he has fake documents?"

The FBI agent gave a quick nod. "It's a possibility, but again, we have feelers out to the known dealers. It would have to be an insanely good forgery and from what we know of Hargity, he doesn't have the money or the contacts."

That was a slight comfort. "Someone must have seen them. Norah is a tall woman ...and Hargity is maybe only one or two inches taller. It wouldn't be easy for him to move her around if she's ..."

God, he nearly said 'dead.' Jesus. The FBI agent took pity on him. "Mr. Conti, look. We're working every angle. We know who took Ms. Reddy—that's a big thing. We know it's not a ransom thing."

"Which is what scares me. If he's keeping her alive ...what's keeping him from killing her when she doesn't do what he says?"

The FBI agent couldn't answer him. "I'll leave you alone for a moment."

Giacomo sat and brooded. *Whatever you need to do to escape him, Norah, do it. Whatever it takes. I swear, I will never hold it against you.*

Just come home to me.

THE PAIN WAS BECOMING OVERWHELMING. Norah sat on the toilet and peed, feeling her insides churning and cramping. When she got up, there was blood in the bowl. "Fuck," She whispered and had to steady herself against the cool tile wall to stop from fainting.

"Norah? You getting on okay?"

"I'm just going to shower."

"Fine."

God, such a bland, normal, everyday conversation to be having with your kidnapper and abuser. She cranked on the shower and left it to get warm, stripping off her dirty clothes. She felt wretched in them and decided to wash them. There were robes on the back of the door. She plugged the tub and let the shower water fill it as she washed herself, her hair, and her body. She saw a trail of blood snaking down her leg and prayed it was just her period. She would tell Lucian it was ...he had always been squeamish. Maybe she could get him to leave her alone for a few minutes while he got her some tampons? Maybe ...

She used the other half of the complimentary soap to wash her underwear, jeans, and top, then hung them over the shower rail. She wrapped herself in the robe and combed her hair through. There was a blister pack of aspirin on the sink; she threw three down with some water and felt better.

"Noh? You done?"

It was a weird feeling—so many times, when they had lived together, she'd heard him say that. It was both strange and upsetting. How had they come to this? She slid from the bathroom and he looked at her in surprise.

"My clothes were dirty," she said shortly. "I had to wash them."

His eyes swept over her robed body and she knew what he was thinking. God, it made her feel sick. "I have my period," she said and it wasn't without satisfaction that she saw the lust in his eyes die.

"God." He looked disgusted. "I suppose you need some tampons?"

She nodded and half-smiled at him. "That would be nice. Thank you."

Lucian's face softened at her smile. "Anything else, baby? Anything that might make you feel better?"

She could almost believe the tenderness in his voice. "Some new underwear might be good. Deodorant. And toothpaste?"

He half-laughed. "So practical. Fine, fine, and how about some candy?"

Despite herself, she nodded. "Red Vines, please. And some bananas. I don't want to ask too much."

That got him—he was starting to believe she was softening towards him. "I will have to cuff you up, though, Norah. I'm sorry."

She shrugged. "I figured. But, please, for comfort's sake, can I be left in the bathroom? You know how it is."

He hesitated for a moment, then nodded. "Sure."

WHEN HE'D GONE OUT—TO her amusement, wearing a comically bad blonde wig under his baseball cap—she looked around the bathroom for any weapon she could use. The top of the toilet tank was heavy porcelain. She could lift it, but she wasn't sure if she could swing it. A couple of tiles were loose. If she pried them off, she could use them to cut his throat while he slept. She kicked the bath surround, but it seemed to be solidly built. Standing on the toilet, half-crouched because of how she was cuffed, she could just about see through the small window. Outside, it was dusk, and all she could see was thick forest and the edge of the motel sign. She poked at the glass of the window, but it was set fast. She clambered down and sat on the toilet lid. Her eyes lit on the towel rail and she put out her hand and grasped it. It wobbled in her hand.

Loose. Her heart started to beat faster. She studied it and found that one end had loose screws but the other was stuck fast. She tried to turn the nail with her fingernail and her fingernail ripped off painfully. Norah cursed and looked around for something small and thin. Nothing. Fuck.

Maybe she could find a sliver of tile. She tried that, managed to pry a little piece off, and tried to use it. It snapped in her hand.

She glared at the towel rail, then grasped it with a growl and shook it violently to jerk it free. It didn't budge. Panting, Norah was about to try again when she heard a car outside. She frowned. That was quick. Then she grinned. Yeah, it was quick ...which meant they weren't far from civilization.

She was sitting back on the floor when Lucian came in. He smiled at her. "You're going to love me when you see what I got."

She blinked. Did he really just say that? But, seconds later, she forgot everything when he held up a bag of steaming hot fast food. "I got way too much, but I figured what the hell."

He uncuffed her from the radiator and brought her into the bedroom. She almost swooned when she saw him pull out a foil-covered burger. "With everything, the way you like."

They'd been living on crackers and potato chips. He handed her a cup of ice-cold soda. Sugar. "Oh, my god, so good." She couldn't help but sink her teeth into the burger, still steaming hot and oozing with ketchup and mustard. Lucian watched her with a smile on his face. She nodded to him. Keep him sweet. "Thank you, Lucian. I appreciate it."

He looked delighted. "Also," he held up a packet of Red Vines. "And I got you some new underwear, some blue jeans, and a couple of t-shirts. Also the toiletries you wanted."

"Thank you."

Lucian grinned. "Maybe we could watch a film together? Relax?"

She nodded, careful not to seem too co-operative. Lull him into it. Now he thought she was on her period, she could get away with not ...god, she didn't even want to contemplate sleeping with him, but if that's what it took ...

As they watched the movie—some dumb action film—she was noting everything in the room she could use as a weapon. Lucian kept looking at her and she didn't want him to grow suspicious. She leaned her head against his chest to hide her eyes from him and continued her stock take. Lucian might be be stupid, but he'd removed anything she could potentially grab—ashtrays, glass jugs, anything. She sighed. The towel rail or the toilet tank lid were still her best bets.

By the time the film was over, Norah was exhausted. Whatever was going on inside her was draining her energy and she lay her head down on the pillow and closed her eyes. She felt the bed shift as Lucian got up. She heard the toilet flush a few minutes later and then the bed dipped as he lay down beside her. She kept her eyes shut as he kissed her mouth.

"I love you," she heard him whisper. She kept up the pretense of being asleep and it was only when she heard his snores that she opened her eyes and stared at him.

I hate you. I hate you, and if I get the chance, believe me, Lucian, I will kill you.

TARA LIT one cigarette after another, sitting out on her balcony. Norah Reddy was alive and Lucian—god, the stupid fucker actually believed he would have a happy-ever-after with her. Jesus.

Tara had been fretting all day, ever since the FBI had come to see her. She had no doubt that Giacomo had sent them to her. They had asked her questions about Lucian and their affair. Did she have any contact with him?

She'd given a command performance. Luckily, after the last call with Lucian, she'd dumped the burner phone she used to talk to him. God bless the sense that had made her use one in the first place. If the FBI had gotten hold of that, they would have found not only Lucian's number but the hitman she'd hired to kill Carmel Price. Fuck, what a mess. She should have told her contact to kill Norah a long time ago,. Then none of this would be happening. Damn you, Lucian.

If she could just find him then she would end Norah herself —and Lucian. Make it look like a murder-suicide. She allowed herself a fantasy of that for a second, then pushed it away. Lucian was wise to her; he wouldn't ever tell her where he had Norah.

So …what to do? She sat, lost in her thoughts when it came to her. She could have laughed out loud. So simple. Deflect and protect.

Tara picked up her phone and called her agent.

THEY HAD DECIDED to meet at The Anthology, and use it as a base. Fred, her distress at Norah's abduction making her unusually subdued, brought them all coffee from the place a block away. Zulika hugged her. "Are you okay?"

Fred shook her head. "I want to kill him, Zul, with my bare hands. The fucking wanker."

Zulika nodded. "There's a pretty big queue."

Fred lowered her voice. "How's Giacomo doing? He looks terrible …for him, anyway."

"Not good." Zulika sighed. "I knew he loved Norah …but even I didn't realize how much. If she …doesn't come back, I don't think he'll survive it."

She suddenly felt a wave of light-headedness come over her and she swayed. Fred gently steered her into a chair. "Have you slept at all?"

"Not much." Zulika had to admit she felt wiped out and Fred frowned at her.

"Dude, you've been sick. You have to pace yourself. Here, have some of this." Fred handed her a hip flask and Zulika grinned.

"Seriously?"

Fred snickered. "It's just orange juice, I swear. You need the sugar hit."

Giacomo and Orlando came in. Zulika noticed Giacomo didn't look at the floor where Norah's blood had stained it. Her heart ached for him.

"I'm just frustrated," he was saying to Orlando. "It's as if they've disappeared off of the face of the earth."

Fred was switching the big-screen T.V.. on—it was an automatic thing now. She hit the mute button so they wouldn't have to hear about nothing new over and over.

Giacomo's phone rang. "Yeah?" He listened for a while, the others silently waiting for him, then he gave a frustrated sigh. "Well, okay, take the net wider. Yeah, Fresno. Anywhere you can think. What? What about her?"

They watched as his expression changed from frustrated to angry. "You have to be kidding me. Which channel?"

Fred, reading his mind, handed him the T.V. remote and he flicked over. "Okay, I got it. I'll call you back."

They all watched as Tara stood at a podium. Giacomo turned the sound up. "As a friend of Mr. Conti's, and of late, of Ms. Reddy's, I do feel it is my job to advocate for them. Please, if you have any idea on Norah Reddy's whereabouts, please get in contact with the police. Her life could depend on your information."

"What the actual fuck?" Zulika was on her feet, but Giacomo held up his hand.

"Wait."

They watched as Tara, dressed in a conservative navy dress with a white Pilgrim collar, looked down as if she were trying to control her emotions. When she looked up into the camera, there were tears in her eyes. "I have to confess something. I feel it is my fault that this has happened." She drew in a long breath. "Almost a year ago, when I was engaged to Mr. Conti, I had an affair with a man called Lucian Hargity. Yes, the suspect. I don't know what I was thinking. I have regretted it ever since, but Lucian, if you are watching, please. Don't punish Norah for my mistake. Please ...bring her home. Thank you."

Giacomo was frozen in disbelief. Zulika put a hand on his arm. "You and Tara were engaged?"

He gave a strange laugh. "No. At no time."

Orlando made a disgusted noise. "What the fuck is she playing at?"

"She's making it all about her," Giacomo said in a flat voice. "Cazzo cagna ..."

Zulika looked between the two men. "Will it help or hinder the case?"

"I don't know which way. If she pisses Lucian off ...god."

Giacomo was grim-faced. "If Norah dies, I'll make Tara's life a living hell."

NORAH COULD FEEL HERSELF FADING. The pain in her stomach—really her whole body now—was keeping her awake, and no matter how many aspirins she took, it wasn't getting better. Lucian was beginning to notice. "You still got cramps?"

She nodded. She figured if she told him she was badly hurt, he would kill her rather than take her to the hospital.

Three days. Three days since she'd been taken, but it felt like a lifetime. Her mind was foggy and when she looked into the little mirror in the bathroom, she barely recognized herself. Her usually golden skin was a sickly yellow and there were huge dark circles under her eyes.

Now she was feeling so sick that she lay down voluntarily on the bed to sleep and closed her eyes. Sleep evaded her, but when Lucian suddenly cursed loudly at the television, she sat up and took notice.

She watched in disbelief as Tara performed for the cameras. Lucian was angry. He looked around at Norah. "Can you believe this bitch?"

She couldn't help the words as they shot back at him, "Well, you fucked her. Surely you would have known exactly what she was like?"

For a moment, she thought he was going to lose it and regretted her words. Her body couldn't take another attack. But then, to her surprise, he looked shamefaced.

"I don't know what I was thinking, Norah. She can't hold a candle to you."

Norah felt tears in her eyes. Don't feel badly for him, you crazy woman. She looked away. "Doesn't matter anymore."

She lay back down and closed her eyes, but the hot tears flooded through them anyway. Lucian obviously saw her shoulders shaking because he was at her side in a flash. He uncuffed her hand from the bed frame and cradled her in her arms.

Norah didn't know how any coherent thought got through to her—all she could think was lLet him hold you. This is your chance to convince him, to get his guard down. She didn't fight him as he held her against his chest.

They stayed like that for nearly an hour before Lucian's phone rang. He let her go and sat up, sighing.

"What do you want, Tara?"

Norah was suddenly desperate for a pee, so she pointed at herself and then the bathroom. Distracted, Lucian nodded and waved his hand. Norah walked slowly, as if her brain wasn't working at a hundred miles an hour. She peed, then as she was washing her hands, she listened to Lucian arguing with Tara.

. . .

Lucian cursed at Tara. "What the hell was that farce on the television? You think I won't tell them about you? About what you did to that lawyer?"

Tara laughed. "Fuck you, Lucian. I told you to kill that whore and you not-so-politely declined. These are the consequences. One thing ...just thought you should know ...I know where you are."

Lucian ended the call, cursing and banging on the bathroom door. "Norah, come on. We have to go."

There was no answer. Shit, was she okay? She hadn't been looking so hot. Lucian banged again. "Norah? Baby, you okay?"

When she didn't answer, he opened the door to find ...nothing. What the fuck?

He yanked the door wider and he saw her. He saw her in the final second before the towel rail she was holding crashed down on his skull and knocked him senseless.

Norah didn't waste a second. She dropped the towel rail and ran. The motel room door was locked, but she knew that if she hunted for the key, Lucian might wake up and then she'd be a dead woman.

She picked up a chair and threw it through the window. It smashed into a thousand pieces and she crawled through the hole, ignoring the glass which cut into her skin. And then she was out.

"Hey!" She heard someone shout behind her, but ignored him. If it was the manager, Lucian's buddy, she knew he wouldn't help her.

She ran barefoot across the rain-soaked parking lot and into a clump of trees. She found herself in a small campground. An unattended tent sat nearby, and without thinking, she darted in, looked around for anything she could use—a cell phone or a weapon. Nothing. A small torch was all she could see and she swiped it and headed out again.

The motel had been halfway up a small mountain and now Norah pushed forward through the thick trees, ignoring the searing agony of her body and the harsh ground on her bare feet. The adrenaline carried her through as she ran—ran from her certain death. All she could think of was getting back to Giacomo.

She couldn't tell if it was her imagination, the adrenalin coursing through her, or the fear, but the sounds of pursuit were all she could hear. The rush of the trees and the brush around her as she ran, stumbling in the near full dark. The tiny torch bobbed and weaved, barely helping her at all. She fell, her body slamming against the ground and her ribs against a tree stump, agonizing pain shooting through her. The torch flew from her grip. She lay still, listening. She hadn't imagined it. She could hear his breathing close, so close. A twig snapped less than a foot from where she lay. Then she heard it—the whisper.

Norah, Norah, Norah ...

The urge to scream was overwhelming, but she didn't move, even closing her eyes in case what little light there was caught them. The world stopped turning.

Then he was gone. For a second, Norah couldn't believe it, but then she scrambled to her feet, panting with terror. In a few minutes, she scrambled out onto the road and saw a Chevy truck. She ran toward it, but saw the cabin was empty. She tugged on the door and it opened. With a choked laugh of delight, she saw the keys were in the ignition.

Somehow she managed to put her foot down, screeching away from the mountain and away from Lucian. Her mind couldn't process the fact she was still alive and her flight instinct took over, not caring if she was speeding or weaving all over the road. She prayed that a cop car would come along, that she would be stopped—even arrested. At least she would be safe. Now that the energy from the escape was leaving her, the pain returned and she moaned as she fought off the lightheadedness. She had no idea where she was, so she just kept driving until she began to see road signs.

Fresno. She almost burst into tears, so relieved she was still in her home state. I'm coming home, Giacomo ...

But the pain was getting worse and she desperately tried to fight off the dark spots encroaching on her vision. She heard the sudden screech of a police cruiser's sirens and then the tears did come.

Thank you, thank you.

She pulled the truck over and got out just as the deputy approached her. "Ma'am, are you okay? Ma'am?"

Finally knowing she was safe, Norah did the only thing she could and collapsed, unconscious, into the deputy's arms.

GIACOMO WAS OUT DRIVING AROUND, as was his normal night now. He knew it was pointless and that he'd never find her like this, but he had to do something. The rain was getting heavier, though, and visibility was poor. He drove around for an hour or two, then went home. The apartment rang with emptiness—with the ghost of her. Every room seemed to remind him of something about her, about them, and about the two of them being so in love. The kitchen where they would cook together after work, or try some new cordon bleu recipe on the weekend, to varying degrees of success. The living room—a place of comfort, of relaxation, and very often the place where their lovemaking would begin before moving to the bedroom.

He closed his eyes, imagining her here with him now, her

gentle touch, her fingertips tracing down his cheek, and her soft lips against his. The feel of her slender body under his and her legs around his waist. That moment when his rock-hard cock would push into her velvety cunt and she would sigh with happiness.

Norah ...Norah ...

He was jolted out of his reverie by both his phone ringing and his head of security knocking furiously, then, not waiting for for permission to enter, bursting in. Giacomo stood, his phone to his ear as the man nodded at him. Adrenaline coursed through his body. His security man nodded, smiling broadly.

"They've found her."

CHAPTER FIFTEEN

Zulika's breath was coming in short gasps as she, Orlando, and Fred raced through the hospital corridors. As they turned into the relative's room, she saw Giacomo, his head in his hands, and her heart nearly failed. But then he looked up and smiled, and she saw genuine relief and joy in his eyes. He hugged her.

"She's going to be okay. She's in surgery at the moment, but the doctor's say she should be fine."

Zulika could feel the tension in Giacomo's body. "What aren't you telling us, Jack?"

"Sit down, all of you, and I'll tell you."

Zulika kept a hold of his hand and Giacomo squeezed it. "He beat her. Badly. The docs say she has a splenic injury and she's been bleeding internally for a couple of days. Luckily, it wasn't a huge rupture, or she'd be gone. They're doing a repair now. The rest of her injuries are still horrific, but they'll heal."

"Have you seen her?"

Giacomo shook his head. "Not yet. They had to take her straight into theater. She escaped ...she got free herself. She had to steal a car, but a police cruiser stopped her. Once they realized who she was, they rushed her to hospital. She's back, Zul. She came back to us."

Zulika burst into tears and Giacomo laughed softly. "That was my reaction when my head of security told me. I think I might have freaked him out."

Orlando hugged his best friend and grinned. "That'll do it every time. God, brother, I'm so happy for you. For us all."

Giacomo nodded. "The police don't really know much yet. She wasn't in the condition to tell them. Except for one name. Lucian."

"Well, we kind of guessed."

"Yeah."

"How long will she be in surgery?"

Giacomo shook his head. "I don't know. I just know I can't wait to see her."

NORAH OPENED her eyes and for a moment, all she could feel was relief that the pain had gone away. Her body felt heavy though, and as she moved, her muscles protested. She sighed and she heard a chair move. Then he was there, her beautiful love, and he was all she could see.

"Il mio prezioso," Giacomo's smile was so full of love that Norah felt all the tension in her body leech away.

"Giacomo...ti amo."

His lips found hers, but it was a gentle kiss—a tender kiss. "Thank you for coming back to me, my beautiful Norah."

She felt his tears on her cheeks and her fingers stroked his dark curls. "Always, my love, always."

There didn't seem a need for words, not for the moment. Norah wrapped her arms around his neck, and Giacomo half-sat, half-lay with her. Neither of them saw Zulika look around the door, smile, and quietly back out, closing the door to give them the privacy they deserved.

LUCIAN, his head screeching with pain, was on the run. He had stolen his manager's buddy's car and headed north, trying to get to Oregon. He almost made it.

Tara and her henchmen caught up with him at the border. He'd risked checking into a cheap motel under a false name, but one of the staff there recognized him, and at dinner at the adjoining diner that night, had mouthed-off to one of her friends that she was going to call the police on him and get a reward. Unluckily for her—and Lucian—one of the detectives Tara had hired was sitting in the next boot.

LUCIAN STOOD underneath the shower for a long time, washing away the blood that had turned his hair red and thinking of the moment Norah had knocked him out. When he'd come around, saw the broken window, and realized she was gone, he'd given a howl of rag andpanic. He'd plunged into the forest, knowing she had only one way down the mountain and, for a brief time, thought he had seen her in front of him. He stopped and listened for breaking foliage and heavy breathing. He whispered her name, hoping that if she was hiding nearby it would freak her out enough for her to blow her own cover.

Nothing. Norah was gone. He knew Tara would be even more apoplectic that he'd kept Norah alive and then lost her. Plus, the police would be on his ass. Fuck. How the hell did it get to this?

He finished his shower and dressed in the thrift store fatigues he'd stolen earlier that day. Attempted murder, kidnapping, actual bodily harm, burglary, theft ...they were going to throw the goddamn book at him. He had just sat down on the bed and flicked the television on when the door was kicked in.

Tara's men grabbed Lucian and shoved him against the wall. Tara herself followed them in, her eyes cold, her beauty icy and terrifying.

"You stupid fuck," she said. "You've found every way to fuck up my life, your life, and everyone's life. You should have killed Norah when I told you to."

Lucian wasn't stupid. He knew there was only one way this was going to go down, so he had nothing left to lose. "Fuck you, cunt."

Her smile was chilly. "You did that, remember? Not that it was memorable—ever. Seriously, Lucian, I have to know. How did you ever, ever think Norah would come back to you? She would leave Giacomo Conti for you?"

He smiled back without humor. "Well, it worked for you."

Tara paused. "And that was my mistake. Yours was not putting a bullet in Norah. A mistake that I will almost certainly have to rectify myself."

He sneered at her. "You mean with one of your goons? The great Ms. Tara Hubert would never get her own hands dirty."

Tara gave a small laugh. "That's been your problem all along, Lucian. You underestimate women. You underestimated Norah and you underestimated me. I'm almost tempted to give Norah her happy ever after out of sheer admiration ...except for the fact that it would mean her winning. And she doesn't get to do that."

"Don't hurt her." *Really? Now you're concerned about Norah's health? What does it matter anymore?*

Tara held out her hand and one of her men put the gun into it. She pressed the muzzle against Lucian's forehead. "Sorry, Lucian. I'm going to have to make sure, now, that she dies a really slow, really horrific death. Painful. If you had just done what I said ..."

Lucian closed his eyes. Norah, I'm sorry, I'm sorry, I...

TARA PULLED THE TRIGGER.

WHEN NORAH HAD RECOVERED ENOUGH to talk to the police, she was more than willing to tell them everything. Giacomo was with her for most of it, holding her hand and trying not to wince as she described the horrors of what had happened to her. Norah, though, was determined that both Lucian and Tara would pay for what they did.

"Obviously, I can't prove it," she told the detective, a tall, handsome African-American called Hollister Bean, "But I would stake my life on Tara Hubert having something to do with Carmel Price's murder. If she could just order my murder because I got in the way of her being with Giacomo, she may well have tried to hide her affair with Lucian the same way."

Det. Bean nodded. "It's certainly something we should look into. It might explain that bizarre press conference she held. That pinged our radar immediately."

Giacomo smiled grimly. "I can assure you, detective, nothing she said in that statement was remotely accurate. We were never engaged. She was never Norah's friend."

"Don't worry, we believe you. Ms. Reddy, this might be a delicate matter, but the doctor's say there was no, um, evidence of sexual assault. Is that correct?"

Norah nodded and glanced at Giacomo. "No, Lucian did not try to force himself on me, this time, at least. It was strange. He actually thought that by being nice to me, he could get me to respond to him. I knew that my only chance was to play along with him. Thankfully it never got to the point where I had to make a choice to …go that far." She drew in a deep breath and looked again at Giacomo. "But I would have done anything to get back to you. Anything."

She studied him as he nodded. He didn't look away or seem angry.

"I understand, mio caro."

She didn't know why it was important that she tell him that; after all, she hadn't slept with Lucian—hadn't had to, thank god. But she wanted him to know she would have done everything to get home to him alive. How much she would sacrifice for his love. Giacomo touched her cheek tenderly.

Det. Bean nodded, watching them. "Well, after you escaped, we think he tried to pursue you but gave up. The motel room where you were held was emptied, but we found a helluva lot of forensics. We're alerting every field office in the country. We'll find him."

"What about Tara?"

"Obviously we'll bring her in for questioning, but unless we can definitively tie her to your abduction, or Mrs. Price's killing …"

"Lucian will testify against her," Norah was convinced. "They aren't on the best of terms and he's such a coward. He'll roll on her, I guarantee it."

The detective nodded and, pushing his chair back, stood to leave. "I'll update you as soon as we know everything. In the meantime, Mr. Conti, I see you have arranged security for Ms. Reddy and yourself? I think that's a good idea. Until we have either Miss Hubert or Mr. Hargity in custody, I would consider staying somewhere neither of them knows of."

Giacomo nodded and Norah thanked the detective. When they were alone, Giacomo sat on the side of her bed, careful not to jostle Norah. Her surgery had been a keyhole procedure to repair the spleen rather than remove it, but she was still in pain.

She clicked the morphine medication button now.

"Does it hurt very much, mio caro?"

She smiled at him. "Enough that it's distracting me, and the only thing I want to think about is you."

He smiled and kissed her. "I love you so much, Norah Reddy."

She pressed her lips firmly to his. "And I you, Giacomo Conti." She leaned her forehead against his. "I know they're still out there, but something inside me says that we're almost home clear, you know? That there's nothing we cannot overcome as long as we love each other."

"I agree. And to that end ...the doctor's say you'll be recovering for a few weeks yet. So maybe it's a good time to start planning our wedding. I need you to be my wife. I need to be your husband. It's that simple."

She grinned. "I'm with you. What were you thinking?"

Giacomo laughed. "Bella, I'm a guy. All I want is to shout out to the world that the most brilliant, beautiful woman in the world somehow wants me. But, still, City Hall is also fine."

She chuckled. "You know what I'd like? I'd like to get married in Italy, with Zulika, Orlando, Ferma, and your family. I want to meet your family, my love."

Giacomo smiled delightedly. "Then that's where we'll do it. My family is spread all around the country, but I do own a house in the Tuscan hills. We could get married there if you'd like. Perhaps when you are released and are well enough to travel, we can go there for your recuperation."

"That sounds heavenly."

He moved so he could put his arms around her. "I promise, only good things from now on, Bella."

. . .

ZULIKA WAVED goodbye to Ferma as the child skipped happily into school. She had offered to take the girl, as Orlando had been called to a meeting in the city. As she walked back to Anthology, she felt tired. Now that Norah was and safe thought she might be able to relax and sleep, but still she was haunted. In her bones, she felt exhausted. She had an appointment with her oncologist later in the week and her instinct was telling her that he would not have good news. How could he? She'd never been so dog-tired in her life and she was sure her cancer had worsened.

Fred greeted her with a smile when she got to work, and despite herself, Zulika felt better. Fred had been her rock and her comfort at work since everything had happened. "I honestly don't know how we coped without you," she told her young friend now.

Fred rolled her eyes. "Don't give me that. You've been like family to me."

Zulika smiled and went into the back room. Family. Strange how life worked out. To Zulika, her family was not the one she grew up in, but rather the one she had found later. Norah. Orlando and Ferma. Giacomo. Fred.

But maybe, just maybe, there would be a link back to her past. Her step-father had called her, distressed—well that was an understatement—devastated over Lucian's spiral into this desperate situation. Zulika had always had a distant but respectful relationship with Peter Hargity. She'd taken his name when her mother had married him, but after her death, the two of them rarely spoke, communicating mostly by Christmas card or email.

Peter had always treated her mother well, so Zulika should not have blamed him for Lucian's behavior, but somehow she felt as if there had been something missing in the man's relationship with his son, something that triggered Lucian's obvious personality flaws.

So when he had called and asked to come and see her, she had –agreed—mostly because she wanted to get some answers. Her step-father knew nothing of her illness and she didn't particularly want to inform him.

She called Orlando now and told him, and he immediately offered to be there with her. She was grateful. Ever since Norah's abduction, they had seemed to grow closer—not as lovers, but as ...she hesitated to use the word ...partners. As if the horror of the kidnapping had reminded them both that life was short and to spend it with the people whom you loved.

She hoped her step-father would find that kind of peace too.

HOLLISTER BEAN FELT every day of his fifty-eight years. He steered the car into the motel parking lot and parked. He remembered coming to this island with Deana for a day out the year before she had died. She'd loved all the farm shops and the small town feel of the place. He didn't blame his old buddy, Doug, for moving here and getting away from the city, but he could never do it. Hollister was a 'Frisco man—a city man. He lived for the heady, frenetic pace of the homicide department, the growl of the city's underbelly, and the fact no day was the same as the another. Doug was now the police chief on this island on the Columbia River. When he'd called Hollister this morning and told him they had a body that matched Lucian Hargity's description, Hollister hadn't hesitated. He had gotten in his car immediately.

As he got out, he noticed Doug across the road in a coffeehouse. Hollister looked at the Old Movie House's impressive façade, the old marquee offering up promises of fine coffee amongst friends. He smiled slightly at the mock film titles: To

Kill a Mocha-Bird; The Sheltering Chai; Americano Psycho. He locked the car and walked over, pushing open the door and smiling at the pretty dark-haired girl who called out a greeting to him. She was talking to Doug, who turned and smiled at his old boss. Hollister wasn't one for hugs, but seeing the strain on his friend's face, he made an exception. Doug clapped him on the back and introduced him to his pretty friend, Noor. Hollister refused her offer of coffee.

'Thanks, but I'd sooner get to the scene if it's okay with my young friend here.'

Doug walked him back to the motel, leading him to a room at the far end of the lot. Already, the place was teeming with crime scene specialists. Doug made an annoyed sound in his throat.

'I asked them not to disturb the body. Let's hope they haven't. The word of a small-town chief doesn't carry as much weight as a homicide cop."

Hollister looked sideways at him, a small smile playing around his mouth. 'Missing the power, Doug?'

Doug grinned ruefully. "Some." A bored-looking medical examiner was leaning against the outside, making notes. Doug nodded at him and turned to Hollister. 'I'd like you to go in alone for a sec, take a quick look, then come out. First impressions.'

Hollister nodded and walked into the motel room. Flies rose and a miasma of scavenging automatons swarmed around Hollister as he approached the corpse. He vainly batted a few away, the sheer number of them making his action redundant. The man's body was at the end of the room, spread-eagled on the floor. A huge hole in the man's forehead was already seething with maggots. The smell was overwhelming, the scent of decay and putrefaction hitting the back of Hollister's throat, making him gag. He covered his mouth with a handkerchief and got closer. A bullet straight to the T-zone. Instant death. Lucian Hargity's eyes were open, staring, his face contorted in agony, and his mouth stretched out in a silent scream.

Vomit rose in Hollister's throat. He stepped back, trying to avoid the blood that covered the cheap linoleum. He reached the door of the room and stepped into the mercifully fresh air. After a minute or two, he sucked in great lungfuls of oxygen. Doug stood watching, a tired, knowing expression on his face. The M.E. looked between the men curiously. Hollister nodded at him. 'You can go in now.' He waited until the doctor had gone in, then pulled Doug away from the motel room and the stench and horror. Hollister looked at his friend, his gaze resigned.

'Yeah,' he said. "It's him."

ZULIKA CREPT into the room to grab a blanket. Giacomo, lying next to Norah, lifted his head.

'Hey,' he whispered. 'Are you sure you don't mind us taking over your apartment? I feel badly that you're sleeping on your own couch.'

After Norah was released from the hospital after ten days, Giacomo had wanted them to go to a hotel—anywhere that Tara wouldn't know—but Norah wanted somewhere familiar. His place was out, as was Orlando's (if Norah's suspicions about Tara's involvement with Carmel's murder were correct). Zulika had offered them her apartment without hesitation. Tonight she had intended on staying at Orlando's, but she and Norah had been chatting so much that it had gotten way too late. Now Giacomo apologized again for invading her space.

She rolled her eyes. 'Please.' She smiled and went out into the living room. Giacomo, having made sure Norah was fast asleep, followed her out.

"She okay?"

He nodded, but looked strained.

Zulika touched his arm. 'Hey, she's safe. She's alive. She's mending. Stop beating yourself up. This was not your fault.'

Giacomo slumped into the armchair and shook his head. Zulika sat opposite her friend, concern on her face.

"It's him. He did this. He's the only one at fault here. Well, him and that ...God I can't think of a name bad enough for that bitch of an ex-girlfriend of yours. Crusty skank womble." She looked pleased with her invention.

Giacomo grinned. 'See, there you go. I knew you had it in you.'

Zulika smiled, but then was silent. "The thought of Tara wanting to kill Norah ...I can't bear it, Giacomo." Her eyes filled with tears and he got up and hugged her.

'I know. It defies explanation. But that's the difference between her and us. There's a part of me that believes, really believes, that she isn't human. How the hell did I ever get involved with her?' Giacomo sat on the arm of her chair, his expression confused. For a moment he was silent. He looked up when he heard a noise from the bedroom. Zulika squeezed his arm.

"Get back in there, soldier."

He nodded. "Thanks, Zul."

When he'd gone, closing the door quietly behind him, Zulika pulled the blanket over her and rested her head on the arm of the couch.

Today, although she hadn't told anyone, her oncologist had confirmed her fears. The cancer had spread. She had been calm, nodded, and asked him about treatment options. More surgery. More chemo.

She hadn't had time to process it yet and now she found she didn't want to. Don't wallow. Just deal with it step-by-step, and it'll be okay.

Her cellphone bleeped with a text message. *How you doing, kiddo?*

Orlando. She smiled. *Feeling a smidge like a third-wheel. Otherwise, good.*

I can come get you. Ferma's at yet another sleepover. I swear that girl has more friends than I have hairs on my head.

Zulika giggled. *Then I accept …but I'll take a cab.*

No way. I can be there in twenty.

Zulika hesitated, then laughed softly.*Okay …but I'll come down. Norah's asleep*

Gotcha.

FIFTEEN MINUTES LATER, she had scribbled a hasty note to Norah and Giacomo and, sneaking back into her bedroom, she managed to grab her washbag and a change of clothes. Norah and Giacomo were asleep, Norah wrapped protectively in Giacomo's arms, and Zulika couldn't help watching them for a few minutes. They looked so contented, so together, that it made Zulika's heart hurt. The only time she felt like that was …

With Orlando. She knew then that she was lost, that she loved him completely, and when she saw his email as he drove up to the sidewalk outside her apartment, she knew she had to tell him.

She got into the car and he leaned over to kiss her cheek. She deliberately moved so that she could kiss his lips. He looked surprised, then responded, his fingers coming up to cup her face.

"Zul?"

"I'm tired of waiting, Orlando. So tired. I mean no disrespect to Carmel, I promise you …but I'm in love with you. I think I have been from the start."

He opened his mouth to speak, but she shook her head.

"Please let me finish this before I chicken out. Lando ...my cancer has spread. Now, it's not hopeless by any means, but there is a risk I might not make it. I want to be upfront about that, and so if you have any doubts—any doubts—I can get out of this car right now and we'll call it even. I don't want to put you through that pain again if you feel anything for me like I feel for you. So, cards on the table. I love you and I want to be with you. I might have limited time left. I don't know."

By the time she finished speaking, her voice was shaking. For a long moment, Orlando gazed at her, then quite deliberately started the car. Zulika took a shaky breath in and he smiled at her.

"Let's go home, baby," he said in a low, tender voice. "Let's go home."

BACK AT ORLANDO'S HOUSE, no words were needed. He led her straight to his bedroom and began to strip her slowly, kissing every piece of exposed skin. Zulika shivered with pleasure as she felt his mouth on her clit, his tongue teasing her. Yes. Yes. This was right. This was meant to be.

Orlando lifted her onto his bed and stripped quickly, Zulika admiring the thickly muscled arms and shoulders, the slim hips, and the firm thighs. She reached down to stroke his already hard cock and heard his soft groan as she touched him, cupping his sensitive balls.

"Zulika, you are my love," he murmured and she smiled through her tears.

"I love you so much, Lando. So, so much."

He thrust his cock deep inside her and she wound her legs around his waist, willing him deeper and harder into her, her fingernails digging into his back as they moved together. They made love slowly at first, then as the intensity between grew, with a kind of feral need. Something had been forged between them and they were clawing at each other, desperate to consume as much of the other as possible. Zulika moaned his name as he fucked her harder, his fingers caressing her clit as his cock slammed into her cunt over and over. She gave herself over to him completely, every part of her body on fire. When she came, she cried out his name, losing herself completely in the moment with absolute pleasure, absolute love.

They fucked again, Zulika on top, almost straight away, continuing until both of them were exhausted and panting for breath. They lay facing each other, Orlando brushing his lips against hers. "Zul ...I think it's time to tell Ferma about us. I think she'll be okay. I really do. She adores you."

Zulika smiled. "I hope so ...but I need to make it clear that I'm not replacing her mom. I could never, would never try. But I do love Ferma. I hope Carmel would have approved."

"She would, baby, I swear." He sighed then. "Of course, we will have to run the gamut of her relatives."

Zulika nodded. "Listen, after my relatives, they'll be a cakewalk."

Orlando smiled, but three hours later, when the police came to tell Zulika that her step-brother was dead, they were no longer laughing.

"LUCIAN IS DEAD." Norah softly repeated it to herself again as she dried herself after taking a long, hot shower. She could barely believe it herself. The whole world had seemed to shift on its axis when the police told her and Giacomo, as if her life before Giacomo had never existed and that Lucian, the man they were talking about, had been a stranger to her. She felt relief for herself, sadness for what might have been if Lucian hadn't gone off-the-rails, and concerned for Zulika.

Hollister Bean was coming to see them in an hour and Norah didn't know how to feel. They had precious few details other than Lucian was dead.

WHEN HOLLISTER TOLD them Lucian had been murdered, Giacomo and the detective exchanged a glance. "Tara?"

"We think so. We have a warrant out for her arrest, but to be honest, without Lucian Hargity's evidence ..."

Giacomo cursed under his breath, glancing at Norah. "Then it's settled. We're leaving the country. I'm taking Norah to Italy for the rest of her recuperation."

Hollister nodded. "I think that's a good idea."

Norah's hands were tingling with unease. "What about Zul? Or Orlando and Ferma? If what we think is true, they're not safe either."

Giacomo sighed. "We'll talk to them. Obviously I can't make them come with us. If they don't want to, then I'll make sure they have the best security in place."

Hollister nodded. "Good plan. I think you, Norah, are still in the greatest danger—you and Giacomo. If she's as psychotic as we think ..."

"She is." Giacomo sounded angrier than Norah had ever seen him. His eyes had a dangerous intensity to them and his brow was deeply furrowed. He looked beautiful and terrifying at the same time—an avenging angel. "When you find Tara, let her know from me ...I will never stop trying to bring her down."

LATER, Giacomo drove them back to their apartment to pack for Italy. As Norah emptied the chest of drawers, she looked deep in thought.

"What are you thinking, mio caro?"

She looked up and gave him a smile. "I was just thinking how Tara is at the root of everything. If she hadn't cheated on you, we might never have met in the first place."

Giacomo nodded, but his face was serious. "Possibly. But I like to believe we would have found our way to each other."

Norah smiled. "I think so too."

Giacomo put down the stack of t-shirts he was about to put in his case and took her in his arms. "Principessa, I'm certain of it. God, Norah," he stroked her long hair back over her shoulder. "There would be no life without you. None."

"Right back at you, handsome."

"I can't wait to be your husband, mio caro."

She grinned. "You might regret that; I'm a terrible nag."

He chuckled. "Well, I know that already."

She laughed and leaned into his body. "How long did the doctor say until we could ...?"

She trailed off with a knowing look in her eyes. Giacomo chuckled. "Bella, we have to be strong for the next month at least. I don't want to risk your health."

She grumbled and he grinned. "Although ...there are other ways we could enjoy ourselves that wouldn't involve too much strain."

He made her lie down on the bed, then pushed her dress up to her hips. Norah grinned down at him. "Where ya going, buster?"

He laughed softly, then his fingers were pulling at her panties and a second later, she felt his mouth on her. "Lie back, Bella. Relax. Let me do the work..."

His tongue lashed around her clit, teasing it until it swelled and became almost unbearably sensitive. Norah moaned with pleasure as her orgasm built slowly and when Giacomo began to slide two fingers in and out of her, she came almost immediately, shivering and sighing. Giacomo moved up so he could kiss her mouth and she kissed him back passionately.

"Your turn." She grinned as her hand went to his fly and she unzipped him.

"Bella, you don't have to—"

"Ssh."

Giacomo ssh-ed. Norah took his cock, already huge and throbbing, into her mouth and trailed her tongue up and down the long shaft. She teased the sensitive tip, hearing his sharp intakes of breath as she worked on him, her hand massaging his balls, and her fingertips pressing into the sensitive perineum to arouse him.

"Norah ...il mio amore ..."

She brought him to climax, his semen shooting deep into her throat. She swallowed him down and grinned up at him. "I love you."

He carefully helped her up and held her close. "Thank you, my love. God, I wish we could lay together properly."

She grinned up at him. "Think of the anticipation."

He laughed and let her go. "That's one word for it."

Two hours later, they were on his private jet heading across the country. Norah was asleep in the little bedroom at the back of the plane, but Giacomo was unable to sleep. He grabbed his phone and headed back into the main cabin.

He called his head of security. "Any news on Tara's whereabouts?"

"We have a few leads, sir. One of my contacts said she was in New York at the weekend. She may still be there, but she's in hiding. She knows the police are after her, but she definitely realizes that if we get to her first ..."

"If we get to her first, take her to the hanger. I want to deal with her myself."

"Of course. We've briefed your team in Italy; they're doing daily security sweeps at the villa."

"Good." Giacomo sighed and rubbed his hand over his eyes. "The one advantage she has is who her contacts are. Where they are."

"Her father was a mob boss, right?"

"Right. Look, just do what you can to keep her and her goons away from Norah."

"She won't get near, boss."

Giacomo prayed he was right.

TARA'S FATHER, George, glared at his daughter as she strode into his home in Chicago. "What the hell kind of mess have you got into now, girl? Murder?"

She waved her hand. "Pa, I am your daughter. I had a problem. I dealt with it."

"With all the subtlety of a wrecking ball."

Tara shrugged. Her father didn't scare her—something he'd always admired in her. She was totally without empathy. George Hubert recognized the psychopath in his daughter and had even encouraged it. But her propensity for not thinking her actions through was beginning to threaten their lives.

"Tara, this is going to take a while to figure out."

She raised her eyebrows at him. "Really? It's such a little thing."

"Let me understand this." George got up. "You fucked a nobody, thus cheating on your rich, good-looking boyfriend. Your boyfriend's best friend's wife catches you out, so you have her killed. Just so happens she's a prominent human rights lawyer. Not very low-key. Then your boyfriend finds out you're fucking this nobody, and to get revenge, he hires the lover's girlfriend. Then he falls in love with the girlfriend."

Tara shifted uncomfortably in her chair, knowing her father was about to get angry. She hated it when he got angry. "You make it sound so ..."

"Petty? Ridiculous? That's because it is, Tara. It is. For the love of God ...why did you kill Lucian Hargity?"

"Dad, they haven't got a case. There's no evidence."

"Except you ran. You don't think that looks suspicious?"

Tara said nothing. She could feel herself regressing back to a sulky teen. Her father sighed. "Here's what we're going to do. We're going to contact the police and offer to fully cooperate with them. If what you say is true, then we don't have a problem, except with the press, and we can work on that."

Tara sat, fuming, but then nodded. "Fine. I'm confident the police have nothing on me but, if I'm going to risk it, I need you to do something for me."

"What?"

She smiled grimly. "Giacomo's fiancée never gets to see her wedding day."

George Hubert glared at his daughter for a long moment, then, almost imperceptibly, he gave a nod.

HER MURDER WAS the last thing on Norah's mind as she walked through the cool stone corridors of Giacomo's Tuscan villa. The place was from a fantasy, she thought, all billowy white drapes at the windows and outside, the Tuscan countryside with rolling hill and olive groves ...

"Heaven," she sighed and Giacomo smiled at her.

"I'm glad you like it."

"Understatement. I think I must be dreaming."

He took her hand and led her inside, to his bedroom. There was a huge four-poster bed with draped white mosquito netting and pure white Egyptian cotton sheets.

But then her attention was solely on the gorgeous man who took her in his arms and kissed her. "I can't wait until I can be with you properly and make love with you all night as we used to. But until then, we can still enjoy each other."

He carefully picked her up and lay her on the bed, pulling at the belt of her wrap dress, then sliding his hands under the material to stroke her bare skin. God, she wanted him so much. She wanted his cock inside her, driving her toward almost unbearable ecstasy. Norah couldn't help feel annoyed once again at the circumstances that got her injured and unable—as yet—to fulfill that desire.

Giacomo looked down at her. "You're frowning."

She told him what she was thinking and his smile faded. "I know, mio amore, I'm angry too. But I thank the stars every day that you're still here—that you're safe."

They lay together in comfortable silence for a time, Giacomo's long, warm fingers stroking her skin.

"Giacomo? If it weren't for Zul and Orlando and your work, I could easily stay here forever."

He laughed. "I know, Principessa. It's tempting, no? But as you say, we have our family back in San Francisco. My work ... eh, I have been thinking of taking a step back anyway and doing something different as a side project."

"Really? What?"

"Something charitable, but I have no idea what yet. I thought we could work on whatever it might be together."

Norah felt excited. "Really? I would love that."

"We make a good team."

Norah smiled at him. "We do."

She felt grateful all over again for this lovely man who had given her so much and who believed in her so absolutely. She rolled onto her side and pressed her body against his, her bare skin against the roughness of his sweater and the denim of his jeans. She could feel his cock thickening as she reached down and cupped it with her hand. She looked up at him from beneath her lashes.

"I can help you with that, my darling."

He grinned and she moved down his body, unzipping his pants and freeing his cock. She swept her lips over the crest of it, hearing his sharp intake of breath as she teased the sensitive tip with her tongue. Norah ran her tongue up and down the long shaft, pulling on it with her mouth until she could feel his orgasm building. Giacomo's fingers knotted in her long hair as he came in her mouth and she swallowed him down. She loved the flush on his face afterward as he panted for air.

"God, il mio amore ...I pray these few weeks go fast ..."

She laughed and kissed him. "Me too, baby. Me too."

16

CHAPTER SIXTEEN

Ferma looked between her father and Zulika and nodded slowly. "Good. Daddy has been lonely and I hate that."

Zulika and Orlando waited for her to say more, but she merely smiled at them. Zulika shot a glance at Orlando before taking the young girl's hand.

"Ferma, I'm not trying to replace your mommy. No one could ever do that. I miss her so much, so I know you do."

Ferma nodded. "I know. It's a separate thing."

Orlando beamed. "When did you get so smart?"

Ferma giggled. "I'm not silly, Daddy. I know that you and Zulika like each other. I told Aunt Claudette that I thought you should be together and make each other happy now."

Zulika felt both happy about Ferma's response and uneasy about Claudette. Although she had always gotten along just fine with Orlando's sister, there still had been a distance too. Claudette was not easily won over, Zulika guessed.

. . .

She asked Orlando later, and he confirmed his sister's stoic nature. "I'm the emotional one in our family," he admitted with a rueful smile. "Claudie has always been the rock, the steady one. But you shouldn't be nervous; she does like you."

"But will she like 'us?'" Zulika fretted and Orlando kissed her.

"Of course she will. She wants me to be happy too."

But, at lunch with his sister later on that week, Claudette raised her doubts. "I'm scared," she admitted, "Scared that because Zulika is still so sick, she won't pull through and that you and Ferma will be right back where you were after Carmel died."

Orlando nodded slowly. "I understand that, Claudie. But Zulika is getting the treatment she needs. She's going to be fine."

Zulika sat in the chair at the oncologist's office and waited to see the oncologist. It had been a few weeks now and tomorrow she would be admitted to hospital for her surgery.

The oncologist smiled at her. "Ready for the big day? I'm going to get all those suckers out. You'll see that I do."

She smiled at his optimism. "Doc, give me the hard truth. Do you think you can get them all?"

He nodded. "Look, I'm not being gung-ho or telling you what you want to hear. From your scans, the tumors are where we can get them and, with a course of chemo I don't see why you shouldn't go into remission. Obviously, there are no guarantees, but I'm very optimistic."

. . .

AT HOME, she packed her overnight bag for the stay, then, on a whim, she called Norah in Italy. It had been a few weeks now that Norah had been in Tuscany and Zulika missed her friend.

"Hey, babe." Norah sounded relaxed and happy and it made Zulika's heart lift.

"Ciao, Bella. How are you?"

Norah laughed. "I'm very good, thank you. Had my last appraisal at the hospital today."

Zulika laughed, knowing what that meant. "Well, I'm glad I called before the orgy began. How's the wedding planning coming along? Have you met Giacomo's family yet?"

"His brother and sister are coming tomorrow. I met his parents. His mom is lovely."

Zulika heard the slight tension in her friend's voice. "And his dad?"

Norah hesitated. "He's hard to read. I'm not sure he doesn't think of me as a gold-digger yet."

Zulika made a disgusted noise. "I hope Giacomo put him straight."

Norah half-laughed. "I haven't said that to Giacomo. It's just the impression I got. I may be wrong. God, I miss you, bub."

Zulika felt a pang. "I miss you too. Hopefully we'll be together soon."

"How're things going with Lando?"

Zulika smiled. "Blissful. But, you know, early days."

"How are you feeling now? Do you have any news for us?"

It was on the tip of her tongue to tell Norah about her surgery, wanting to hear her friend comfort her and tell her everything was going to be okay.

But she knew Norah would want to drop everything and fly back immediately, and there was no way Zulika would deprive her of her time with Giacomo—not after everything they'd been through.

Later, when Orlando got home with Ferma, they cooked together, Ferma holding court about her day and a show-and-tell she had nailed as her father and Zulika moved around each other. Ferma knew about Zulika's surgery and when Zulika went to kiss her goodnight later on, she hugged Zulika tightly. "I know everything is going to be okay, Zully. I just know it."

Zulika had hidden the tears in her eyes as she hugged the little girl.

ORLANDO WAS UNDRESSING as she went into the bedroom. She smiled at him and he took her into his arms. "How're you feeling, baby?"

She leaned her body against his. "Exhausted, I've got to admit."

He pressed his lips to hers and she responded, sighing into the kiss. "Baby, everything is going to be okay."

She chuckled. "Your daughter just said exactly the same thing."

"Smart girl. Takes after her dad."

She laughed and climbed onto the bed, tugging him after her. "Come lay down with me."

Orlando cradled her in his arms and Zulika felt safe in his strong hold. "Lando?"

"Yeah, babe?"

"If anything does go wrong ...or they can't take all the cancer out ..."

"Then we'll deal with whatever comes along. Whatever comes along, Zulika. I love you. Ferma loves you. We are a family."

Zulika realized then that, although she wanted Norah here, both she and her friend now had their person, the love of their lives who would support them and, in turn, who they could lean on. Norah had Giacomo and she had Orlando. Zulika stroked his face now.

"Thank you, my darling. Thank you."

GIACOMO HAD COME from a lunch with his father and his mood was bleak. Although he had suspected some reticence on his father's part about his forthcoming marriage, he hadn't realized the depth of his dad's doubts about Norah.

"I don't understand where she came from," Enrico Conti had told his son. "First she is just the girlfriend of Tara's lover, then she is suddenly your fiancée?"

Giacomo had fixed his father with a cold look. "After everything Norah has been through, you think she has ulterior motives? Really, Papa? You met her—her loyalty, her love, and her sweet nature shine out from her. How can you think like that when you never once accused –Tara—who at this point, might be a murderer—of the same thing?"

His father waved a hand. "I don't believe that for a second and besides, Tara is from our world."

"And what world is that?"

"Wealth. Status. Breeding."

Giacomo pushed his chair back, making a disgusted noise. "Norah is the classiest person I know, Papa, and very soon, she'll be my wife. Do you honestly think money matters to her?"

"It matters to everyone."

GIACOMO WAS STILL THINKING of his father's words as he drove back from Florence. Switching the engine off, he sat in the car for a long moment, trying to get rid of the tension in his shoulders. It was early evening and dusk was beginning to fall. The villa was lit, soft, warm light coming from a few of the windows.

At the perimeter of the grounds, he could see his security guards keeping vigilance. In the evenings, his staff would go back to their own homes after dinner and he and Norah would have the place to themselves.

Norah ...even thinking her name made the tightness in his chest ease, replaced with a certainty. The certainty of love and of destiny. She was his future and no one would ever come between them again.

He got out of the car and went into his home. The villa was quiet, but as he turned into the hallway, the huge staircase to the second floor in front of him, he saw her. She had lit candles and placed them all the way up the staircase, and now she sat, clothed in a simple white dress, her long, dark hair pulled over one shoulder.

"Buonasera, il mio amore."

"Hello, Giacomo. I've been waiting for you."

Norah sat up and slowly spread her legs, pulling up the dress to reveal that she was naked beneath. A smile spread across Giacomo's face.

"You've been given an all-clear?"

"Oh, yes ...now, hush that beautiful mouth of yours, come over here, and fuck me senseless, Giacomo Conti."

He laughed, tugging at his tie, and went to her, his mouth seeking hers. Her fingers knotted in his dark curls. "God, I missed you, Bella."

Her hands were at his fly and suddenly all he could think about was being inside of her, taking her right there, his instincts animal and feral. He pushed up her dress, tugged her legs around his waist, and plunged into her, his hands pinning hers back against the staircase as they fucked, and his cock plunging deep with every stroke, their eyes locked on the others.

"God, I love you, Giacomo Conti ...yes ...yes ...harder, please, harder ..."

Her soft voice spurred him on, his hips slamming against hers, all reason and sense leaving them as they clawed and pulled each other's hair, their lips rough against the other's skin. Giacomo gave a long groan as he came, his cock shooting hot cum deep into Norah's belly as she shivered and moaned. He didn't let her rest, scooping her up and carrying her to their bed. Ripping the cotton dress from her shoulders, he kissed every inch of her skin before flipping her onto her stomach and entering her from behind. He bit down on her shoulder as he fucked her and she cried out with pleasure, his cock filling her. She felt unbearably sensitive as it plunged deep inside her cunt. God, he wanted her in every way, all day, all night,.His rough hands on her soft skin and the sound of her gasps and moans in his ears. Giacomo lost himself in her, fucking her until her cunt swelled and throbbed, then he pushed into her ass, feeling the tightness of her on his cock. Norah called his name over and over, smiling up at him, encouraging him to cum on her skin, and moaning with desire as he shot his seed onto her belly.

"I love you so much," she whispered as he fucked her for the fifth time, her velvety cunt enveloping his cock once again.

"Ti amo," he said, with all the feeling inside him. "Ti amerò per sempre, Norah Reddy. Per sempre." I'll love you forever.

Afterward, she fell asleep in his arms and Giacomo buried his face in her hair, breathing her in. How had he lived before Norah? He couldn't fathom it.

SLEEP FOUND HIM QUICKLY, as he was exhausted from lovemaking, but it was an uneasy sleep. The nightmares began almost immediately.

Their wedding. Thousands of white flowers bedecking the terrace at the villa and all of their friends and family gathered to celebrate them. Norah was an angel in white and her eyes were glued to him, her smile full of joy. She walked down the aisle on Orlando's arm and had almost reached them when Giacomo felt a cold breeze sweep over him and clouds go across the sun. As Norah approached where Giacomo was waiting, a figure stepped between them. In horror, Giacomo watched as the figure pressed a gun to Norah's belly and fired repeatedly. At first, she didn't react, and Orlando seemed not to notice the shooter, but he dropped Norah's arm and stepped away. Then there was no-one there except Norah and Giacomo. He tried to go to her, but he couldn't move, and as he watched, spots of red appeared on her wedding dress. Norah looked confused as the blood began to pour from her wounds. She looked at Giacomo. "But I'm pregnant," she said softly, "I have a daughter ...Ferma ...Ferma, our daughter ...why would anyone do this?"

She crumpled to the floor and the scene was suddenly awash with a wave of blood. All Giacomo could do was open his mouth and scream and all he could taste was death ...

"GIACOMO! Giacomo! Stop ...stop ...it's okay. It was just a dream. Stop. You're hurting me, stop ..."

He opened his eyes and recoiled away from Norah. He had been gripping her wrists tightly, so tightly he could see red marks. He collapsed back against one of the bedposts and sat, panting for air. "God, Norah, scusa ...I'm so sorry."

Norah, her eyes wide and frightened, reached out a hand to him. "It's okay, baby, truly. You were screaming ..."

For a second his mind whirled, and he couldn't make sense of anything. He pressed his fingers into his eyes. "Mio Dio."

Norah sat in silence, waiting for him. Her hand stroked his arm gently. He'd hurt her. He opened his eyes and took her hands, studying her wrists.

"They're fine, Giacomo. Seriously. I'm more worried about

you." Norah gently extracted one of her hands and touched his face. "How long have you been having nightmares?"

He sighed. "They started when you were missing and stopped after I knew you were going to be okay. I have no idea why it's started again."

Norah gave him a small, mischievous smile. "Maybe something to do with heightened emotion?"

His body relaxed then. "Are you sure I didn't hurt you?"

"Absolutely sure. Do you want to tell me about the dream?"

He shook his head. "No, I don't want to think about it."

She crawled over to him and curled herself into his arms. "Then maybe we can do something to distract you."

He smiled down at her fondly. "Insatiable."

"You betcha."

CHZPTER SEVENTEEN

Grayson Harris was used to getting jobs from George Hubert. Hubert called him when he wanted someone dealt with speedily and discreetly, and as long as he was paid upfront, he was happy to do it.

But lately, he had felt a dissatisfaction with his job. The people he was hired to kill ...some of them, he was sure, didn't deserve to be dealt with that way.

And then there was Delilah, his granddaughter and the love of his life. Her chocolate brown eyes and merry nature gave him something he could not describe. A new outlook on life? Maybe, he thought to himself now, as he sat down opposite Hubert. That old cliché, but it was true. She made him believe in good again. Was it too late to redeem himself?

He'd never liked George Hubert, but he knew the other man trusted him to get the job done. It satisfied Grayson that he was the one person Hubert seemed afraid of.

Hubert handed him a manila folder now. "I need it done quickly and discreetly."

Grayson opened the folder and took out the photograph. "A woman?" That was a first—for Hubert and Grayson.

Hubert didn't look comfortable and suddenly Grayson realized that maybe this wasn't a job for Hubert. He knew all about Tara, Hubert's spoiled bitch of a daughter. He would wager any amount of money that this woman in the photo was Tara's ex's new woman.

"Put a bullet in her and I'll make sure you're paid double your normal fee."

Grayson put the folder back on the desk. "I don't kill innocent women."

Hubert sat back, dissatisfied. "Look, normally I wouldn't ask ... triple fee. Come on, man, you don't even know her. She gets lead in her belly and you get rich. How does that sound?"

Grayson stared at him. He looked back down at the photograph. God, she was a beauty. Long, dark hair, curvaceous body ...chocolate brown eyes.

He gazed at the picture for a long moment, then gave his answer to George Hubert.

TARA HAD BEEN QUESTIONED for twenty-four hours and released without charge. She was almost gleeful as she left the station with her father's lawyer, but back at the house, her father merely nodded. "Fine."

"Is the other thing arranged?"

Her father turned cold eyes on her. "Norah Reddy will be dead soon enough. But you, you little whore, you will spend the rest of your life making this mess up to me and to the family."

Tara rolled her eyes. "Whatever."

She never saw her father's hand before it slammed into her face. The force of the blow knocked her out of the chair and onto the floor. Before she could make a sound, her father picked her up and threw her across the room. She crashed into a cabinet of fine china, the glass breaking. She slumped the floor and started to sob, wailing as he approached her again.

He bent down and took her chin between his fingers. "Now, girl, you will start to make this right, so that when Ms. Reddy is murdered, it doesn't come back to us. Because I swear, Tara, I don't give a fuck if you are my daughter ...if you bring this down on my house, you'll meet a fate far worse than she does."

Zulika opened her eyes and tested herself, searching for the pain. She knew she was on a morphine drip, but still ...post-operative pain was a certainty. Yet she felt nothing.

Shit, am I dead? Then she heard voices—familiar voices.

"Zully?"

A child's voice, followed a man's deep, mellifluous tones, calling her name.

Yes, yes, I'm here ...

She blinked and tried to focus as her vision cleared, then she saw them. She saw them and she smiled.

Ferma. Orlando. Both were grinning like maniacs at her, and she knew without being told what the surgeons had achieved.

She was cancer-free.

Orlando had called Norah and Giacomo after the surgery and now he told Zulika that they were coming over for a week to see her. Norah had called and Zulika could tell she was delighted and overwhelmed, even if she remonstrated with Zulika for not telling her about the surgery.

When Norah arrived at the hospital, she threw her arms around Zulika and the two women hugged for what seemed like an hour. When Zulika drew away finally, both of them were crying.

"You look wonderful." Norah sniffed, smiling through her tears and Zulika laughed.

"Yes, we both do rock the snot."

Norah laughed, and Giacomo cleared his throat. "Listen, why don't we leave you two alone and go grab some coffee?" He bore Orlando and Ferma off to the hospital's cafeteria.

"How do you feel? Really?"

Zulika nodded. "Seriously, so good. Better than I have for months. I think that's having the cloud lifted away from me mentally as much as it is physically, you know?"

Norah nodded and grinned. "I do. God, Zul. It's so good to see you."

Zulika studied her friend. "And what about you? You're glowing."

Norah grinned shyly. "All good, I swear. Now, listen, maid of honor, we have some dress shopping to do when you feel up to it."

"I'm there. Have you been to the bookstore yet?"

Nora nodded. "We checked in with Fred this morning. That girl is a force of nature. The place looks great."

Zulika nodded. "Yep, we landed on our feet there."

"When are you getting out of here?"

"A couple of days, hopefully. No later than Friday, thank god."

Norah grinned. "The food that bad?"

Zulika snickered. "No, but you know me …I'm fussy."

"Well, if you're up to it, Giacomo and I would like to take you out to dinner when you get out of here."

Zulika smiled. "In that case, I'm definitely getting out of here as soon as possible."

. . .

Zulika was zipping herself into a beautiful red dress. During her sickness, she had lost about sixty pounds from her already slender frame and now she wanted to get her athletic but curvy figure back.

Orlando, already dressed, was watching her from his reclined deposition on the bed. She grinned at his reflection in the mirror. "You know, you could help."

Chuckling, he got up and came over to her, drifting a fingertip down her bare spine and making her shiver with pleasure. She leaned back into his touch for a second, then decided that was a bad idea as her dress hit the floor and he was carrying her back to bed.

They made love slowly and tenderly, savoring every moment. "We're going to be so late," she murmured, then gasped as he entered her, making long, rhythmic strokes as his cock drove deeper inside of her.

"They won't mind …they're probably doing exactly the same thing as us …"

Zulika laughed and wrapped her legs tighter around his waist. "I bet they are …"

They were an hour late to the restaurant and as soon as Norah saw them she started laughing. "Don't worry …we only just got here too."

The meal was exquisite and the four friends chatted amiably about the wedding. "So you'll obviously let me fly you all over myself, right?" Giacomo looked at his friend, who laughed.

"On this occasion, yes, buddy. I'll let you spend some exorbitant price on flying my family and me to Italy."

"Good. No arguments," said Giacomo in a tone that made Norah giggle.

"See, I let you be masterful one time and you think you can do it all the time."

Giacomo laughed and kissed her cheek, murmuring something into her ear that made her blush.

Norah looked radiant, Zulika thought to herself. Absolutely radiant. She was wearing a white cotton dress which glowed against her dusky skin and her dark hair was pulled into a messy bun at the nape of her neck. God, you two will have beautiful kids, she thought as she looked at Norah and Giacomo, their heads bent close together as they flirted with each other. You were made for each other.

They lingered over coffee, until finally, at just past eleven p.m., Giacomo glanced at his watch. "I hate to be the party-pooper, but I have a meeting at seven a.m."

"Boo," said Norah, but she stood up with him. As they all walked from the restaurant, Orlando put his arm around Zulika's shoulders. Norah and Giacomo stood outside waiting for them.

Zulika never saw it coming. There was confusion, people on the street pushing past them, Giacomo's raised voice, a man who was staring intently at Norah, and then Zulika heard it.

Pop. Pop. Pop.

Her ears rang as she recognized them as gunshots. What the hell? Everything seemed to go in slow motion. Norah jerked backward and as she fell, Giacomo caught her and Zulika saw the blood.

No. No, please, this can't be happening ... There was a buzzing in her ears.

Giacomo cradled Norah in his arms, sobbing, his hand pressing down on the bullet wounds in her belly. Norah's eyes were closed and she didn't respond when Giacomo screamed her name. Zulika saw the shooter—the killer—disappear into the crowds. People were screaming and already she could hear sirens, but it was her best friend's face she couldn't take her eyes from. Norah.

Norah. Wake up.

Orlando, his face a mask of horror was crouched next to Giacomo and his stricken love, begging Norah to be okay. Zulika fell to her knees. Giacomo looked up at her. "I can't wake her up."

His voice was broken. Zulika felt useless. Numb. Paramedics were there then. That was fast.

"No pulse."

No. No. Don't you dare die, Norah. Not now ...

"Let's get to her to the E.R."

In a taxi cab following the ambulance, Orlando's arms tightened around her.

The emergency room chaos. Please let her be okay ...

HOURS OF SURGERY. Hours.

The surgeon coming to see them. The sadness and regret in his eyes.

No. No. This isn't real.

BUT IT WAS REAL.

Norah was dead.

GEORGE HUBERT LISTENED to the message, then put the phone down and went to find Tara. His daughter was in her old bedroom, wearing old sweats, no make-up covering the bruises on her face. He felt no sympathy for her.

"It's done." He said to her and she nodded.

"Good."

George sighed. "No, I mean it's done. The girl's dead and so is our relationship. You destroyed what was left of my patience, Tara. Get your stuff. Hugo will drive you back to the city. I don't want to see you again."

He left his daughter staring after him and walked back to his study. It had been a long time that he had known Tara was a liability. So now he'd had enough. She had enough of her own money. She wouldn't suffer. He just hoped she kept her head and stayed away from Giacomo Conti.

Because George Hubert was one hundred percent sure his daughter would not survive that encounter.

AT SIX A.M. THE following morning, Giacomo came to get them, his face blank. "Come with me."

He led them down into the basement halls of the hospital, passed steam pipes and shadowy closets. He asked them to follow him into a room that was poorly lit, and at first Zulika, her eyes swollen from crying, didn't see him. When Giacomo flicked the light on, she blinked, then recoiled for a second. "You son of a bitch!"

It was Norah's killer. Zulika lost her senses and flew at him, her fingers outstretched to scratch his eyes out.

"Zul, stop."

Zul froze and then turned to see her best friend—her dead but somehow very much alive best friend—step out of the shadows.

"What the fuck is going on?" Orlando looked as shocked as Zulika. Norah took Giacomo's hand and Zulika could see she was trembling.

"I'm sorry we had to put you through last night, but we needed it to look real. For everyone else." She nodded at the 'killer.' "This is Grayson Harris. He was hired by Tara's father to kill me. He chose another path."

Zulika felt the energy drain out of her and she sank into a chair. "Why? Why not go to the police?"

Grayson Harris half-smiled. "I'm afraid that's my fault, or rather, my ...old occupation's job."

Zulika stared at him with cold eyes. "Why should any of us care if you're arrested, Mr. Harris?"

"Because he could have just taken George Hubert's money, killed Norah, and gotten clean away." Giacomo's voice was calm, but there was a tiny break in it and Zulika softened.

"Right." She turned back to Norah, who was watching her with a wary look in her eyes. "So ...why the charade?"

"We need Tara to think Norah is dead ...we need her to show her hand. We think she's hiding out at her dad's place, somewhere we can't get to her. If she thinks Norah is dead, she might try the whole 'lean on me' thing. She'll come out of the woodwork or whatever and then we'll have her." Giacomo looked at Orlando. "Lando ...Grayson found out something you should hear."

Orlando blanched, obviously guessing what he was about to say. Carmel's murder ... He faced Grayson, his gaze intent on the other man. "Just tell me ...was it you?"

Grayson stood. "No. I don't kill women. I swear that to you. I'm very sorry for your loss—to be honest, I was somewhat of a fan of your wife's, as bizarre as that might sound for someone like me. I didn't kill her." He looked at Norah and smiled. "I would not have killed you either, Ms. Reddy. But you know that."

"I do." Norah gave a nervous laugh. "Excuse me, but this whole thing is just bizarre to me. Still."

Zulika walked over to her and wrapped her arms around her. "I understand why you did what you did—and great acting, by the way, both of you—but man, when this is all over, I'm opening a can of whoop ass on you, buddy."

Norah laughed and hugged her. "I don't blame you …it was pretty grim."

"Even the surgeon and emergency room staff were in on it?"

"Amazing what funding a new wing of the hospital will get you," Giacomo smiled and Zulika nodded.

"Right."

Orlando cleared his throat. "So how is this going to work? I mean, you can't just walk out of here. The paparazzi are already baying for blood out front."

Norah nodded. "I'm going to be a master of disguise."

"Really?"

"No," she grinned at him. "I'll be wearing a surgical mask and scrubs. It really is that complicated. Then I'll get a cab to a hotel and camp out there for a few days until we see how the land lies."

Giacomo slid his arm around her waist. "Not too long, Principessa. And if it's safe, then I'll sneak in."

"So what now?"

"Now, we'll just have to wait."

NORAH OPENED the door of the hotel room a crack and chuckled. "You just couldn't stay away, huh?" She opened the door, pulled Giacomo inside, and locked the door again. He caught her mouth with his, lingering over the kiss. Norah slid her hands under his t-shirt.

"You're overdressed, Mr. Conti …"

He pulled his t-shirt over his head in one move and she laughed. "More like it."

"Uh-ah, your turn …" He pulled the spaghetti straps of her dress down her shoulders and let the dress slip to the floor,

"Hmm. Still not naked enough." With one quick move, he unclasped her bra, and her full breasts fell into his hands. He dipped his head to take each nipple into his mouth in turn. Norah sighed, closing her eyes and reveling in the sensations his tongue sent shivering through her body. She tangled her fingers in his hair, breathing in his clean, woody scent.

"Giacomo ..." she whispered and he stood and covered her mouth with his. He lifted her easily in his arms and carried her to the bed. He kicked off his jeans and underwear and made Norah laugh by taking the waistband of her panties in his teeth and attempting to pull them off.

"You lunatic," she gasped with laughter and pushed him away, sliding her underwear off. Giacomo straddled her and she grinned up at him. "What are you looking at, mister?"

Giacomo grinned. "Well, for starters, the most exquisite face on this earth." He bent over and trailed his lips across her cheek to her mouth, "The most delicious lips ..."

Norah sighed as his lips pressed against her throat and down to her breasts. "Each perfect nipple ...'

His hand drifted between her legs and began to caress her clitoris. Norah gave a soft moan, and Giacomo chuckled, his laughter rumbling through her belly as he found her navel and began to run his tongue around the edge, circling it. He slipped his finger deep into her cunt and began to slide it in and out of her. He kissed a path from her belly down to her sex and took her clit into his mouth, sucking it gently and teasing it with his tongue.

Norah groaned and writhed as he pleasured her, gasping his name and coming hard as Giacomo moved up the bed and plunged his diamond-hard cock into her. "Mio Dio, you're beautiful ..."

Norah smiled up at him. "I love you so much ...oh god, Giacomo ..."

He chuckled as he began to thrust harder, enjoyed the undulations of her body beneath him, her large, ripe breasts pressing into his chest, and her soft belly trembling with desire. He sought her mouth again, massaging her tongue with his, and feeling her fingernails digging into the muscles of his back.

He came explosively, groaning, calling her name out over and over, and shooting thick creamy cum deep into her belly. Norah, her cunt hot and clenching around his cock, bit down on his shoulder and gave a long, drawn out moan of pleasure.

"Baby, remember when we used to fuck in your office? With the door unlocked?"

Giacomo grinned. "How could I forget, you little exhibitionist?"

Norah laughed as Giacomo lay down by her side, both catching their breath. "Well, earlier, I was exploring this hotel and do you know what? They have a rooftop."

Giacomo propped himself up on his elbow. "You don't seem to understand this whole 'keep out of sight' thing, do you?"

Norah laughed. "I was careful. Besides, no one saw me. Anyway, I was thinking ..."

Giacomo smirked. "Dirty girl."

Norah pressed her body against his. "Well, if it doesn't appeal ..."

Giacomo considered for a long moment and his cell phone buzzed. "Hold that thought, mio caro." He grabbed his phone and read the text message. In an instant, his face changed from playful to a fierce triumph. He looked at Norah, his eyes blazing. "Guess what?"

"What?"

"Tara took the bait."

. . .

TARA SAT in the hotel restaurant, idly flicking through her text messages. Or should I say, old text messages, she thought. Her friends had drifted away from her of late and she was sure they all blamed for Norah's murder; they had been friends of Giacomo too before he split with Tara and now they had chosen sides.

Well, who gives a shit? Tara wasn't at all bothered by their disloyalty; she had her career and her money—and now she was finally free of her father and his bullshit. Maybe she should re-hire that dude to kill her father.

She was lost in thought, waiting for Giacomo to show up, when the maître d' appeared by her side. "Miss Hubert? I have a call at the front desk for you."

Really? "Who is it?"

"Mr. Conti, I believe."

Why hadn't he called her cell phone? Tara sighed, got up, and followed the maître d' out to the reception. He indicated a phone just inside the office. Tara walked in and picked up the phone.

"Hello?"

"Boo, bitch." Norah's voice was hard.

Shocked, Tara didn't have time to respond before someone grabbed her from behind and a needle was stuck into her neck.

ZULIKA HAD KISSED Orlando before he left the house, on his way to meet Giacomo, Norah, and the very captive Tara. Zulika looked up at him. "Don't do anything …I mean, if she tries to …" She couldn't get the words out and he gave her a half-smile.

"Just say it plain, kiddo."

Zulika drew in a deep breath. "Stay …you. You are better than her."

He kissed her cheek. "I promise. Even if she acts up." His

face got serious then. "But I can't tell Giacomo or Norah what to do. If they want Tara dead ..."

"Then it's their decision ...but I cannot imagine Norah going for it."

Orlando studied her. "Tara killed your brother. You have as much to say to her as anyone. I could get a sitter for Ferma."

Zulika shook her head. "Lucian was dead to me the minute he raped Norah. I want Ferma to feel safe in her bed."

Orlando kissed her softly. "I love you, you know?"

Zulika smiled up at him. "I do know. Ditto."

Orlando laughed. "Girl, you've been watching Ghost again. Ever get sick of it?"

"Hell, no. Hurry home to me."

"I will."

18

CHAPTER EIGHTEEN

Tara opened her eyes. Tied tightly to a hard wood chair, she blinked in the cold light of the hanger. The air was cold and the private jet stood silently in the huge building. She recognized it immediately. Conti-One. She'd flown on it many times. She wasn't surprised to see who her captors were. Her eyes fixed on the woman who sat on the desk opposite her.

"You just won't fucking die, will you?" Tara's speech was slurred and, humiliatingly, she felt a gob of drool spill from the side of her mouth.

Norah smiled coldly. "Oh, I will. Just at the end of a long, happy life with Giacomo, instead of when a spoiled, bratty, little bitch like you decides it's time."

Tara smirked. "I swear you must have a magical vagina. Lucian wouldn't kill you when I told him too. Giacomo is like a dog on a leash. I should have gotten ..."

She trailed off when she saw Orlando step into her field of vision. "Should have gotten ...the same man you hired to kill my wife to kill Norah?"

Tara was silent. She glanced around to see Giacomo watching her, his fury all too evident and his green eyes dark with anger. She studied him, this man she used to love ...wait ... did she really ever love him?

Yes. God, he was beautiful. All that glowering menace, that hard body, and his huge, masterful cock. Fuck ...why had she cheated on him with that skid-mark Lucian?

She looked back at Norah. Tara knew, in her heart, that she would never match up to Norah Reddy in any department; beauty, brains ...courage.

She looked away from Norah's steady glance. "I suppose this is where you kill me and dispose of my body? You," she nodded at Orlando, "I can see it in your eyes. The rage. The need for vengeance."

Orlando's expression was like stone. "So, that's an admission, then? You had my wife, my pregnant wife, murdered?"

Tara clamped her mouth shut. Giacomo walked over to her, and despite her bravado, she shrank back in the chair.

He put a hand on each arm of her chair and leaned in so his face was inches from hers. "You would think that," he said softly. "You would automatically assume that we brought you here to kill you. Because that's your go-to, isn't it, Tara? Murder. You had Carmel killed because she found out about you fucking Hargity. You killed Hargity because he wouldn't kill Norah. And you tried to have my beautiful girl killed out of sheer spite."

He pinched Tara's chin between his fingers. "We are not like you, Tara."

She jerked her chin away from him. "Fuck you, Giacomo."

He smiled a chilly, icy smile. "You wish, you little bitch. So here's what's going to happen. We're going to deliver you to the police. You're going to admit everything and take your punishment. Or ..."

He glanced around at Norah who nodded. "Or you can walk free from here."

Tara blinked. "What?"

"You can go free."

She started to laugh hysterically. "Fuck you people. Have the balls to take your revenge."

Giacomo half-smiled. "Oh, we already are. Your name is poison now. Every contact you have will no longer take your call. Every contract is now null and void. No restaurant will take your booking, no fashion designer will hire you to walk in their shows, and no magazine wants you on their cover. Ever."

Tara sneered at hum. "I don't believe you. They still have to sell their product and who does that better than me?"

Giacomo looked over at Norah and winked. She beamed back at him and Tara laughed. "Her? She doesn't have what it takes to do my job."

Norah chuckled derisively. "Yes, the capacity to stand up straight and walk somehow eludes me."

Giacomo gave a genuine laugh then before looking back at Tara. "Norah doesn't have to whore herself out like you, but, funnily enough, they were interested in the story of the beautiful girl who survived, the gorgeous woman with a brain the size of Sicily and a heart of gold. Think about it, Tara ...who would they rather have? The washed-up ice queen who treats people like crap? Or the warm-hearted heroine who escaped a madman and is about to marry the luckiest man in the world?"

Norah hopped off the desk and came to stand next to him, linking her fingers with his. Tara watched them, her eyes narrowed.

"So, Norah will be taking over all your commitments before retiring from 'modeling' to do, you know, actual work."

Norah chuckled, looking up at her love. "So bitchy."

Giacomo kissed her. "I know. I couldn't resist."

Tara spat at them. "God, you make me sick."

Norah turned to her. "You know what, Tara? I would never trust a man who hurt a woman. Hit her. As much as both Giacomo and Orlando would love a freebie at kicking your ass right now, neither of them would stoop that low. Me, on the other hand ...I grew up in a trailer park." And she slapped the other woman hard, once, across the face. "Well, now, that was fucking satisfying."

She grabbed the back of Tara's head and forced her to look at her. "Don't ever, ever mess with my man, my family, or me again. Do you understand me? Or I will happily, happily do time for ending you."

Tara recoiled from the growl in Norah's voice and felt a grudging admiration. "You know, my dad's going to be pissed that his guy took the money and didn't kill you."

Norah burst out laughing. "Oh, you moron ...your dad already knows. His 'guy,' as you call it, told him he wouldn't do the job and never took his money. Giacomo went to see your father and ...well, baby, do you want to tell Tara what her daddy-dear told you?"

Tara felt her heart begin to clench and tighten. Giacomo was obviously enjoying this.

"He said he didn't have a problem with Norah living; that he only hired the 'guy' as a last favor to his about-to-be-disowned daughter. Said it wasn't worth his while to keep his promise. Your dad couldn't give a crap about you, princess."

Norah smiled. "And to my mind, that makes ...precisely zero people who do give a crap about you. So what we're offering is the best you're going to get."

Tara laughed then. "What the fuck are you offering? Prison or destitution?"

"Yup."

"That's it. But you get to live, is the point we're making, I think."

Orlando cleared his throat. "Unless, of course, you want to tell us who killed my wife and where to find him?"

Tara smirked. "And lose the only card I have left?"

Orlando stepped towards her, but Norah stopped him. "Allow me, Lando."

Tara tried to scream in the second before Norah's fist smashed into her temple and knocked her cold.

GARBAGE. Garbage and gulls and grime. Tara opened her eyes. She was dumped on a landfill site. She stood up and clambered down of the pile, gagging and heaving all the way. A couple of raggedy dumpster divers stared at her, but she ignored them. Her clothes and her hair were soaked in old, stinky food and god knows what else.

It wasn't until she finally tumbled to the bottom of the trash pile that she saw them.

Paparazzi. And every single one of them was laughing at her.

SIX WEEKS later

AS THEY SAT outside the café on Florence's sun-drenched streets, Enrico Conti read the newspaper silently as his son and Norah waited for his reaction. Tara's picture was still headline news, even after all these weeks. Her broken contracts, her fall from grace, and now she had disappeared. Norah couldn't rustle up any sympathy for her.

She watched her future father-in-law from the corner of her eye. Since they'd returned to Italy, she'd spent even more time with Giacomo's lovely mother, Vittoria, his sister. Adriana, and occasionally his brother, Enzo, but his father had still kept his distance. He was certainly polite to her and she thought he might be thawing, but no sooner than she thought she'd made progress, he would retreat again.

Giacomo had assured her that his father wouldn't stand in the way of them marrying, and now, with the wedding a week away, Norah couldn't feel anything but optimistic about the future. In two days, Orlando, Zulika, Fred, and Ferma would be arriving, and then she and Zulika would be frantically trying to organize everything.

She was regretting not having some gelato, as the weather was so warm, but she felt too relaxed, Giacomo's arm around her, to bother asking for some now. Giacomo and Enrico were chatting about something in Italian now, and although she was picking up the language, she didn't listen along, instead just people-watching.

Norah fiddled with the coffee cup as the two men spoke. She tried not to keep glancing at Enrico Conti, trying to read his reaction to her. She felt as if there was a little thawing, but he was so hard to read, she couldn't be sure.

The sun was beating down on Florence, bright on the café's windows, and at first, she could not believe what she was seeing until the woman came closer.

Tara.

The blonde woman, her face unmade, her hair bedraggled, lurched towards them, her gaze fixed on Giacomo who had his back turned towards Tara.

"Giacomo!"

All three of them stood, people around them scattering as Tara raised the gun and pointed it at Giacomo's chest. "You ruined my life, you bastard."

Giacomo was calm. "No, Tara. You ruined your own life."

The gun was shaking in her hand, but Norah saw her flick off the safety. No. No way. Without another thought, she shoved Giacomo hard, right into his father, as Tara fired the gun. Norah felt a sting in her shoulder, but the adrenaline had kicked in and she dived at Tara, knocking the gun away from her.

"Get off me, you bitch." Tara was scratching and clawing at the other woman, but Norah was in no mood to be fucked with. She slammed her fist into Tara's face over and over, all of her pain, her guilt, and her anger fueling her. It took both Giacomo and his father to pull her off the other woman. Giacomo wrapped his arms around her as two polizia came running to help.

Norah couldn't recall what had happened next; the red mist in her brain was so virulent, so overpowering, she felt like she was a gibbering ball of rage. Every ounce of pain, hurt, betrayal and fear came out of her as soon as she'd seen Tara point that gun at her beloved Giacomo, and she knew that even if Tara killed her, she would not let Giacomo die.

She finally calmed down as the doctor examined her shoulder. Giacomo was holding her other hand and his father stood a way back, watching the scene with that unreadable expression of his.

"It's just a flesh wound, thankfully," the doctor said finally. They had been surprised to find an American doctor working at the Florence hospital's emergency room. "You won't even need surgery."

"Good. With respect, doctor, I've seen the inside of a hospital too much recently." Her voice was scratchy and she felt Giacomo's lips pressed against her temple.

"I'll numb the area and we'll get you cleaned and stitched

up. Now, how do you feel in yourself? The bullet didn't do the damage, but the shock could affect you."

Norah shook her head. "No, I'm fine, doc, I promise. I'd rather be with Giacomo than in here. If I relapse or anything, I'll come back."

The doctor nodded, seemingly satisfied. "Well, hang out here, Supergirl, and we'll get you cleaned up."

Norah closed her eyes and leaned against Giacomo. "It's really over now, huh?"

They had seen Tara dragged away by grim-faced polizia, and later the chief inspector had assured them that Tara would be facing a raft of charges. "The F.B.I. have also reached out to us. Mr. Conti, perhaps you would like to speak to them when you have a moment."

Giacomo reminded them of this now and excused himself to go call the agency. Norah sat in silence, suddenly feeling uncomfortable with Giacomo's father.

Enrico Conti pulled up a chair and sat next to her. To Norah's shock, he took her hand and she saw tears in her eyes.

"What you did today," he said in broken English. "You saved my son. You put yourself in harm's way for him."

"Of course I did, Enrico," she said softly. "I would die for Giacomo. Happily. Willingly. As he would die for me. I know you think I'm some opportunist, latching onto the nearest billionaire. I honestly don't give two craps about his money. It's his money. I make my own way in the world. Yes, sometimes the things he wants to do are out of my pocket, but we balance that out. Money is nothing in comparison to time. The time I spend with him. With our friends. With his family. That is more precious to me than any amount of money."

Enrico smiled at her. "I believe you, Norah Reddy. I am sorry I was so ...reticent? Is that the word?"

She grinned. "It is. Your English is better than you know.

And never apologize for protecting your son. Although the circumstances weren't great, I'm glad I was able to show you how I really feel about him."

Enrico stood and bent to kiss her cheek. "I must tell you ... even before today, I was beginning to change my mind about your motives. Goodness shines from you, Norah."

Norah flushed scarlet. "That's a lovely thing to hear. Thank you."

"I speak only the true."

She grinned. "Truth."

Enrico chuckled. "I speak only the truth. I will have to spend more time with you to improve my English."

"I would like that."

Giacomo came back then and she saw the happiness on his face when he saw them laughing together, but he didn't mention it. "The F.B.I. just told me that the hitman who killed Carmel rolled on Tara in exchange for a lesser sentence. She's going away for the rest of her life."

Norah gave a little gasp. "God, I'm so happy for Orlando and Ferma. Closure, at last."

Enrico nodded, smiling, and excused himself. Norah knew he was giving them some privacy.

Giacomo nodded, sitting down beside her. "I called Orlando ...he's pretty happy. He's even letting me fly them all over in the jet."

Norah blinked. "Wow. We're really getting married in less than a week."

Giacomo touched the wound on her shoulder. "The battle-scarred bride."

She grinned at him and pressed her lips to his. "You betcha. I'll wear this scar with pride, my love."

His smile faded and he took her face in his hands, his eyes

serious and intense. "You saved my life today. Again. You are my miracle, Norah Reddy."

He kissed her slowly and tenderly, pouring all his love into the embrace and ignoring the amused looks of the nurses who wandered in and out, and of the doctor who came to stitch her wound ...

THE END

ABOUT THE AUTHOR

Mrs. Love writes about smart, sexy women and the hot alpha billionaires who love them. She has found her own happily ever after with her dream husband and adorable 6 and 2 year old kids.
Currently, Michelle is hard at work on the next book in the series, and trying to stay off the Internet.
"Thank you for supporting an indie author. Anything you can do, whether it be writing a review, or even simply telling a fellow reader that you enjoyed this. Thanks

©Copyright 2021 by Michelle Love - All rights Reserved
In no way is it legal to reproduce, duplicate, or transmit any part of this document in either electronic means or in printed format. Recording of this publication is strictly prohibited and any storage of this document is not allowed unless with written permission from the publisher. All rights are reserved.
Respective authors own all copyrights not held by the publisher.

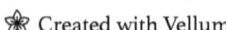 Created with Vellum

www.ingramcontent.com/pod-product-compliance
Lightning Source LLC
LaVergne TN
LVHW021701060526
838200LV00050B/2449